DRY ROT

H.E. GOODHUE

SEVERED PRESS
HOBART TASMANIA

DRY ROT

WWW.SEVEREDPRESS.COM

ISBN: 978-1-925342-94-9

DRY ROT

The streets were full of husks. They were everywhere. Spilling out from alleys and behind dumpsters. Bumping around the sides of parked cars. Climbing through the shattered windows of storefronts. Their withered, leathery skin looked orange under the streetlights. I knew it was gray, but the sodium lamps painted everything in sepia tones. I hate orange and gray. I hate husks more.

One stumbled out from behind a mailbox and lunged for me. It clawed at my jacket with sharp, skeletal fingers, trying to drag me to the ground. Its teeth clacked inches from my right ear, making it ring. I shook myself free from the husk. It looked up at me from the ground with milky, spoiled eyes. Its teeth clicked as it tried to bite the toe of my boot. I stepped back and brought the heel of my boot down on the back of the husk's neck. Wrapping my hands around its spindly neck, I snapped its head to the side. Its body went limp. I could still see it chewing the air. A second stomp scattered the spoiled black jelly inside the husk's skull across the sidewalk. I watched the thick liquid creep towards the curb and into the street. I'm sure it smelled awful. I'm sure I would have puked if I smelled it. Fortunately, my NBC mask kept the stench out.

I expected more blood. This was probably the tenth or eleventh husk that I killed and I still wasn't used to the fact that their blood had thickened, turned to sludge in their veins. I cut them, shot them and now, even stomped on them, and the most it left behind was a disgusting black jelly and sometimes a reddish powder. Then again, I probably shouldn't have been surprised that killing something that was already dead didn't exactly follow logic. Still, I thought there would be more blood.

More husks were coming. I needed to move. What they lacked in strength and intelligence, they more than made up for in numbers and determination. I slipped around the side of a pharmacy. I had shopped here before. It had been one of those nights where my daughter woke up with a fever and I ran out to find something to lower it. Not many pharmacies were twenty-four hours around us, so this one was my go-to spot for late night emergencies. That had been so long ago. Kara was still a baby then. Eleven years later and she didn't really need her father to run out in the middle of the night anymore. I would always see her as my baby though. Age and time didn't matter. She could never be anything other than that. I tried not to think about happier times. Even times with fevers and vomiting were happier than this. At least then we had been together.

A high wooden fence blocked off the end of the alley. A handful of husks had followed me down there. I leapt up and grabbed the top of the fence. My breath fogged up my NBC mask as I climbed onto the fence. I straddled the fence and watched the husks come closer.

They all looked the same. Their bodies were thin, dried out and hardened. Errant patches of stringy hair clung to their scalps. Eyes, dull and lifeless, were set into deep sockets. Sharp edges of bone poked out where the husks' skin had worn away. The tattered remains of clothing hung from the husks like flags of surrender. I hated them. I wanted to kill them all, but there wasn't time for that.

I needed to see my wife and daughter again. That was all that kept me going. It was what kept me going long before the husks showed up.

Kara: Daddy, where are you? I miss you.

I stared at the text message on my phone. It made my head light. I closed my phone and leapt over the other side of the fence. I needed to go home. I needed to see my family.

Two days before…

Gray. For three years now that has been the only color I've seen. The walls are gray. The mattress on the bunk above me is gray. Some days, even the food was gray. How the fuck do you turn meat gray? Hell, the sky looks gray on most days, but then again everything looks gray when you're watching it through chain link and barbed wire.

After a while, even people's faces began looking gray. Maybe it was the food? Or maybe it was the captivity? Either way, after about a year I stopped seeing people. We weren't people anymore, just gray, hollow shells of our former selves. We were ghosts.

About the only thing that wasn't gray were my clothes. Those were orange, bright orange with the letters DOC across the back in black. In the beginning, it seemed almost cruel that we would be supplied with such a bright color to wear. It only served to draw more attention to the fact that everything around me was gray. That was probably the point.

I shouldn't really complain. Some guys had it worse than me. I was only sent here for five years and I was getting out in three for good behavior. There were guys in here that would never see the outside again. Those guys had it the worst and they knew it. If you were never getting out, there really was no reason to be good. What more could they do to them? Going to the SHU or a few days solitary? Sure, those threats were always there, but it never changed anything. The guys that were never getting out, those were the ones you needed to watch out for.

God, Frank is farting again. That gray meat goes right through him and then straight through the mattress. I should have argued more about getting the top bunk. But then again, you have to pick and choose your battles. Top bunk and no farts wasn't really worth getting stuck in the back while I waited in the food line. I don't really think Frank would have shived me, but I'd seen it happen to other guys.

Besides, once you got past the farts, Frank wasn't so bad to share space with. Most of the time we left each other alone or passed the time talking about what we did before we ended up here. Frank had been some sort of aspiring actor. He landed a few bit parts on daytime soaps. He also landed a ten-year sentence for DUI on the freeway. The eight ball of coke in the cup holder hadn't helped either. And me? Well, I had held just about any job a high school diploma could get, which isn't many. But before I ended up in here, I had been working construction, not that I built anything. I was chief engineer of dumpster loading and hole digging. The work wasn't bad. I even missed it some days. I missed my wife and daughter more.

We had a small TV on the steel table next to our toilet. It was made out of clear plastic so we couldn't hide things in it. One time we even caught a rerun of some shitty soap that Frank was in. He showed up for about thirty seconds with a pizza and then someone's evil twin shot him because they didn't have money for the tip or something like that. I don't really remember, but it made Frank happy to see it. I guess it let him know that the outside world hadn't totally forgotten about him.

I think that's probably the worst part about being here – being forgotten. Most guys can handle the shitty food, the showers, the yard, but it's the lack of contact that really gets to them. Once someone stop reminding you that you were once human, it's pretty easy to forget. I kept a picture of my wife and daughter taped to the wall. My old cellmate pulled it down and tossed it in the sink because he wanted to hang up a wrinkled page from some low rider magazine. I didn't mind the picture of the car or the girl sprawled across it, but he shouldn't have touched my picture.

I remember the way his teeth burst from the sides of his mouth as I smashed his face into the rim of the steel toilet. He didn't need many teeth to eat the picture of the car.

He lay on the floor gurgling as I taped my picture back in place. The guards beat on me pretty good and I got a few months added on to my sentence, but it was worth it. You have to hold onto to what makes you human, even if that means breaking another guy's jaw with a toilet.

After that, Frank was moved into my cell. He got how things were. You just didn't touch a picture of a guy's family. It was that simple. Frank was always respectful of those kinds of things. But my god, his farts were terrible. Some nights, I was pretty sure I was watching the drab gray paint bubble and peel on the walls. I guess you couldn't really blame a guy for something he did in his sleep.

No matter though, I was out in thirteen hours. Most guys counted years or months. I was down to counting hours. That made me pretty lucky, but it also made me a target. Those guys that were never getting out hated to see someone who was. If they caught wind of someone's release date, they'd make sure to try and trip you up so you'd have to stay longer. Misery loves company, I guess.

Some asshole stole my Jell-O at dinner tonight, just grabbed it as he walked past. A while ago, that would have been grounds for a beat down. Not that I liked Jell-O. In fact I hated it, but you couldn't let stuff like that happen. But screw him. Tomorrow morning that prick was going to wake up to another day of gray and Jell-O. I was going home.

-3-

Sunlight trickled in through the narrow window set high in the wall of my cell. Even though sunlight came through the window it did little to brighten the interior of my cell. Like I said before, everything was gray. Besides, the window was only about the size of a shoebox and the glass had chicken wire set into it. I'm not really sure who could escape through a window of that size, but they must have had their reasons for putting chicken wire in the pane. Maybe a few of the crack heads or tweakers were skinny enough to squeeze through, but the rest of us sure as hell weren't.

"You gonna miss me, Lucas?" Frank asked as he rolled over and released a toxic blast of gas.

"Are you seriously going to ask that while farting?" I coughed and waved my hand in front of my nose.

"Something to remember me by," Frank said. He climbed off the top bunk. "One more meal and you're home free, right?"

"That's it, man," I nodded. "One more shitty breakfast and I'm gone."

"What are you going to do?" Frank asked. He checked his reflection in the polished sheet of metal that hung above our toilet-sink combo.

"See my family," I said. It was a trite answer, but an honest one. I didn't have any plans for revenge or getting rich, nothing like the other assholes in here. Plans like that made sure you wound right back in here. No, all I wanted was to see my wife and daughter. That was it.

"Nah, man that's not what I meant." Frank walked over to look me in the eyes. His usual demeanor was gone. A look of concern was plainly written on his face.

"Well, what is it then?" I asked. It was my turn to use the sink and mirror.

"In the mess hall, man," Frank continued. "It's your last meal before getting out. Someone is gonna try to mess with you. Trip

6

you up, just like last night. Lucas, you need to be ready for that shit."

"Last night?" I asked. "You mean the Jell-O? Man, fuck the Jell-O. Those idiots can eat my entire breakfast for all I care. I just want out. The last thing I'm going to do is getting into some pissing contest over some powdered eggs."

"Just be careful man, okay?" Frank said. "I know you can handle your shit cuz of all that wilderness survival shit you done, but it's a different type of wilderness in there."

I spat a mouthful of toothpaste into the small basin that sat on top of our toilet. "Frank, this isn't my first time in the mess hall. I'll be fine."

"Yeah man, it's your last time," Frank said. "And you know how the lifers get when someone is on the verge of getting walking papers."

"I'll be okay," I said. "Thanks, Frank."

"Yeah, yeah," Frank grinned. "Don't get all emotional and shit now. If I wouldn't cuddle with you before, I ain't gonna do it now."

I laughed. Frank was good for that. Most of the time it was hard to find something to laugh about when you were inside, but Frank found ways to make things funny. That went a long way.

"So are you gonna go back to doing that survivalist stuff?" Frank asked.

"Nah, I don't think so," I said. "My wife was never really a fan of it. Besides, I've done enough surviving over the last three years." The truth was that I missed the woods, but I missed my family more. My wife, Lisa and daughter, Kara had never been into camping or spending days out in the woods. They humored me from time to time, but building a hut from pine boughs and purifying pond water was a line they would never cross. We had a nice tent and gas stove that I would bring along when they were with me. That was never my thing, but I loved being with them.

My father and two of my uncles had been game wardens in Maine. In those parts, being a game warden was a kind of catch all job. My father tracked poachers and checked fishing permits, but he also handled local business like domestic disturbances and drunks. There weren't any real police, at least not within a hundred-mile radius, so self-reliance was kind of important. This was a lesson he instilled in my two sisters and me.

We spent weekends out in the woods killing things we could eat, sleeping under the stars and learning to live off the land. My dad always told us that civilization was make believe, that something like that could only last for so long before it broke. People, he said, were just animals that had learned to fool ourselves into playing nice. Eventually, we'd remember that the days of smashing rocks over each other's heads were more fun than watching television and when that happened that we had better know what to do. My dad dug out the floor of our basement to build a bomb shelter. We spent damn near thirty hours down there when Y2K rolled around. So maybe he was a little bit paranoid, but that didn't make what he taught us any less true, especially once I got put in this place.

Once I moved down to 'the flat lands' or what's more commonly known as the East Coast, I kept on with what my dad taught me as a kid. It was a nice way to remember the old man, but the truth was that I had never fully accepted that society wasn't one accident away from full on collapse.

Lisa didn't like to talk about that kind of stuff and I made sure not to scare Kara with it. Still, that didn't stop me from digging out our basement. The shelter was huge, but it had three cots, a few respirators and a ton of nonperishable food. Lisa wasn't too happy when she came home from work and found Kara and I in the basement. Kara smiled and pointed at what would be our new 'clubhouse.' After that, I thought I might end up living in our 'clubhouse' but Lisa finally got over it once I put locks on the door and convinced her it was a safer place to keep my guns than that shitty cowboy safe I picked up at Wal-Mart.

I didn't care about any of that stuff anymore. I didn't care if society failed and broke down. Hell, it had been broken for me for the last three years, so what did I care? All I wanted was to see Lisa and Kara again. That was what kept me going for three years. It would definitely be enough to get me through one last breakfast in the mess hall, regardless of what those assholes might try to do.

The door to our cell jumped on its track and clanged into place. The guards started yelling to line up.

"Ready?" Frank asked.

"Stop stressing so much," I said as we walked out onto the platform. One tier above us and two tiers below men in orange suits were doing the same. We put our hands behind our backs and stood in line. The guards paced up and down, checking for any problems. There didn't seem to be any so we started shuffling towards the mess hall. I hoped there wouldn't be any, but Frank's paranoia was making it difficult.

"Watch yourself," Frank said in a near whisper as we moved in a line towards the cafeteria.

"Shut your mouth," a guard barked from somewhere near the doors leading into the cafeteria.

"I'm fine," I said as I grabbed my tray. "Relax, man."

"Yeah, well whatever." Frank picked up his tray and cast a quick glance around the room. Tables, bolted to the floor, were filled with men. A sea of orange writhed with hushed conversations and the sounds of eating drifted above it all. "You're just lucky you got me here to do the worrying for you."

-4-

Frank and I took our usual spot near the back of the mess hall. Prison was a series of rituals and rules. The guards had some, but the inmates had more and those were the ones you needed to follow. Knowing the guards' rules kept you out of trouble. Knowing the inmates' kept you alive. Our table was away from the gangs, they needed more space, so we remained on the edges, trying not to be seen.

"Gimme that." A huge hand closed around my pile of scrambled eggs. He crammed the fistful of eggs into his mouth. Most of the food spilled out the sides and onto the ground. It was the same guy that took my Jell-O the night before. I couldn't remember his name, but knew he was a low-level foot soldier for one of the gangs in D-Block. He was probably trying to prove himself to one of the shot callers. They would send out one of their idiots to do things. Sometimes there was a reason. Most times it was because they were bored and this is what passed for entertainment around here.

"Have at it," I said and slid the tray towards Jell-O.

"You getting smart?" Jell-O asked. He squared his shoulders and tried to look bigger, more intimidating. The truth was we were pretty evenly matched when it came to size, but I had no desire to get into a fight. I just wanted to go home. "Nah, you ain't getting smart, are you? You're trying to be tough. You think you're tough?" Jell-O snatched an apple from my tray and smashed in on the floor.

"Whatever. Man, I don't care," I said. I stood up to leave the table. Jell-O's hammy fist connected with my shoulder and knocked me back into my seat. I wasn't going to fight. I didn't care if this guy beat seven shades of shit out of me. I just wanted out.

Frank was out of his seat before I had a chance to stop him. He grabbed my tray from the table and swung the hard edge at the bridge of Jell-O's nose. Blood exploded from his nostrils and spilled onto the collar of his jumpsuit. It looked like a morbid clown bowtie. Another time I would have laughed, but I was worried about Frank. He was going to have to eat in here tomorrow or whenever they let him out of solitary and I wouldn't be here to watch his back. Still, Frank had been in his share of fights and most guys left him alone.

The flat edge of the tray crashed against the side of Jell-O's head, knocking him to the floor.

The other inmates were out of their seats in a matter of seconds. Their bodies created a wall around Frank and Jell-O, keeping the guards out. The shouting buried all commands to stop or get down. Soon one of the guards on the catwalk would fire a warning shot from the beanbag gun, but for now it was a free for all. Things happened at two speeds around here – painfully slow or incredibly fast.

"Eat the apple," Frank shouted. "Eat it!"

Jell-O looked up at the tray and saw the rage in Frank's eyes. His trembling hand reached out and grabbed a fistful of the pulpy apple mush from the floor.

"Eat it!" Frank said again. Jell-O took a few bites before Frank slammed the tray down on his head. The thick plastic tray snapped as Jell-O's head bounced off the floor. He went limp. A sweet mush of partially chewed apple hung from his mouth in thick ropes. Frank turned to me and smiled. "I don't think that'll keep the doctor away today."

The echo of the shotgun was deafening. All the inmates dropped to the floor and put their hands on top of their heads. Frank and I lay beside an unconscious Jell-O.

"Why the hell did you do that?" I said. My face was pressed to the floor, but I could still see Frank smiling. "I didn't give a shit about that."

"Yeah," Frank said, "but you're going home. I'm still gonna be here tomorrow and then it would be my turn. You looking weak would make me look bad. Besides, look there." Frank motioned towards Jell-O. I couldn't see what Frank was trying to show me.

"Thanks," I said before a guard dropped his knee between my shoulder blades. Beyond reputation, I don't know what caused Frank to attack Jell-O, but I still felt the need to thank him. He didn't have to get involved.

"No problem," Frank coughed as a second guard dropped a knee on his back and slid plastic cuffs around his wrists. "Go see your family." Two guards pulled Frank from the floor and out of the mess hall.

Two more came through the doors with a stretcher to take Jell-O to the infirmary. They strapped him to the stretcher and checked him. I stared at the makeshift knife one of the guards removed from Jell-O's jumpsuit. Frank had seen it. I hadn't. Missing details like that was the difference between life and death.

Frank saved my life. That was the last time I saw him.

"One cell phone. One brown wallet with forty-three dollars and a Subway coupon - expired. One lock-blade knife. One watch, broken. One set of keys on a Sponge Bob keychain." The contents of my life spilled out of a large manila envelope onto the counter. The officer in charge of my release showed little reaction or concern for the things that had once been so important to me. I grabbed my stuff, took my bus fare and signed out without so much as a word. I think someone wished me good luck as I walked outside to wait for the bus, but I couldn't tell if it was sarcastic or not. I didn't really care either way.

Once I was outside, I checked my phone. The battery was dead. I knew that it would be, but old habits died hard and the first thing I would do after leaving somewhere was check my phone. The screen was black and a few spider cracks crept from the left corner. I didn't remember those being there. Maybe the phone had been damaged when I got arrested. I just hoped that it still worked.

The bus stop near the prison was a mess. The bench had most of its planks missing or broken. The Plexiglas walls were shattered or gone. Graffiti covered every open inch of space. Most of it was from former inmates waiting just like I was after their release.

Back on the streets 4 life – Francisco caught my eye.

I knew about eight guys named Francisco inside and any of them could have written it, because every one of them was a repeat offender. That was just how it worked. Prison only made you meaner and less capable of being part of society. Most guys ended up back inside because it was the only place they ever felt like they belonged. But not me. I wasn't going back. I wasn't going to leave some proclamation or prophecy scrawled on a bus stop bench. I was going home.

The bus pulled up. The glass doors slid open and the overpowering reek of urine washed down the steps. Why do buses always smell like piss? But as I got on I saw why.

A homeless man, who easily could have been mistaken for a pile of rags and trash, sat in the back of the bus. It looked like he was arguing with himself or with the bottle that stuck out from the top of a creased brown paper bag.

I paid my bus fare and took a seat near the front. Only a few other people were on the bus. I guess most people find ways to avoid the line that stops near the prison. I couldn't really blame them.

The bus lurched forward and we were moving. It felt good to be outside, but it was strange. I kept looking around, waiting for something to happen. Maybe the homeless guy was making me nervous, but we had more than our share of crazy inside, so I didn't think it was that. Maybe it was just being outside?

I spent the last three years having someone else tell me what to do and when to do it and suddenly making a decision as simple as where to sit on the bus felt overwhelming. I took a couple deep breaths to try and calm myself and immediately regretted it as my throat, nose and eyes were assaulted with the acrid tang of old piss.

The driver fumbled with the knob of the radio. I caught a glimpse of his profile. He looked worried. The bus came to a stop and the driver grabbed the radio.

"Dispatch, this is Green Six," the driver said. Must have been his bus number and the color of this route. At least it wasn't gray or orange. The irony might have been too much to stomach.

"Go ahead, Green Six," the radio answered.

"Is there something going on? I'm getting a lot of static on the radio and everything but the local stations just went dead," the driver said.

"Green Six," the dispatcher said, "are you pulled over?"

"Yes."

"There appears to have been some kind of accident or attack," the dispatcher continued. "Most radio and television stations in or near cities have gone silent. All we're getting is local and it's not telling us much."

"Any word on what happened?" the driver asked. I leaned forward in my seat to try and hear more of the conversation. The driver was trying to keep it hushed, probably not wanting to panic the passengers, but he was doing a pretty poor job of it. I looked around the bus and everyone was either silent or checking their cell phones for information.

"None yet, Green Six," the dispatcher answered. "Finish your route and then check back in."

I hadn't really noticed the sun before. Inside, I tried not to focus on something that was free when I wasn't. But now I saw clouds pass over the sun. Large, greasy raindrops splattered against the windshield of the bus.

"Dispatch," the driver said into the radio. "Any word on this freak storm? I didn't hear anything about rain today."

"It's springtime, Green Six," the dispatcher said. "It's going to rain from time to time."

The driver hung up and put the receiver back in its cradle and pulled the bus away from the curb.

I tried not to let the feelings of unease grow larger, but couldn't shake the feeling that something was going to happen. Maybe it was because the sky had turned gray? I hated that color and thought I was escaping it.

I was wrong.

-6-

The bus continued on at a snail's pace. The streets were flooded with rainwater. At one stoplight, I watched a gutter overflow and wondered what else was escaping besides the storm water. I guess it probably didn't matter much. These streets were drowning in proverbial shit long before this storm.

The bus driver kept twisting the knob on the radio one direction and then the other. Occasionally, there'd be a break in the static, but never long enough for us to figure out what was going on. People on the bus whispered about terrorist attacks and doomsday cults. I stayed quiet and watched the storm. Something about it bothered me. Then again I found that most things were bothering me today.

"Looks like the storm is letting up," the driver said. He turned to smile at me while we waited at a light. I didn't know what kind of response he was looking for, so I just nodded and went back to staring out the window. The driver began to hum and slide his window open to let air into the bus. It did little to combat the smell.

It did look like the rain was stopping. Maybe it was just a freak spring storm? The clouds thinned and I watched a jagged line of blue cut across the metallic sky. It was nice to see a color other than gray.

The bus pulled up to the next stop. It was still two stops away from mine, but the smell of urine and a break in the rain made me anxious to get off the bus. I grabbed the metal rail and pulled myself out of my seat. The driver said something cheery that I ignored and answered only with a wave. People wasted words out here. In prison, you say the wrong thing or too much of the right and you were likely to find something sharp stuck in your gut. I would have to work on my people skills, I guess.

No other riders got off at the stop. It was calming to be alone on the sidewalk. I spent three years with no time to myself. Hell, I even had to use the toilet with another guy in the room.

The rain had driven most people inside, so even as I walked further along there were few people. The blue in the sky continued to break through and few errant rays of sunshine trickled through the clouds. As I waited to cross at the corner, I found my attention drawn upwards. I hadn't seen a free sky in a long time.

A long line of black twisted through the sky like a scrap of ribbon lost to the wind. It twirled and changed directions, but still headed towards me. For a moment, I thought it might be a flock of birds, but as it got closer I watched a large, powdery flake flutter to the ground in front of me.

"What the fuck?" I asked no one as I used the toe of my boot to prod the flake. It crumbled and fell apart like ash. More began to drift down from above.

Clouds, darker than any I had ever seen, moved across the sky. I worried about rain, but as more of the ashy flakes fell from the sky, I knew that fear was misplaced. Something very bad was happening.

I pulled off my sweatshirt and wrapped it around my face and mouth. I didn't know what was falling from the sky, but I sure as hell was in no rush to breathe it in. The sweatshirt wasn't perfect, but would keep some of that crap out of my lungs.

I looked for somewhere to duck into, somewhere to protect me from the ash that spilled from the clouds. This section of town had been run down and near abandoned before I went away and three years had only made it worse. The old storefronts were shuttered or covered with plywood. There was no way I was getting into any of these spots. My best bet was to haul ass and try to catch up to the bus at the next stop. The bus wasn't the best place to take shelter, but it would be safer than standing on the sidewalk.

I pulled my sweatshirt tighter and ran. The screech of tires and shattering of glass echoed down the street. I had a feeling the bus was going to be out of the question.

7

The ash fell to the wet ground and turned into a thick paste. The sidewalks looked like tubes of black toothpaste had exploded across them. My boots sucked and pulled with each step. I kept one hand over my face, holding the sweatshirt in place, and the other I used to dust the flakes from my clothes as I ran.

There were no sirens. I expected to hear police cars or ambulances at any moment, but there was only the sound of my boots and breathing. The blood in my head was throbbing in my ears and making my head light. I hoped that it was just the insanity of my day and not some early sign of sickness from whatever this shit was.

The next bus stop stood on the corner at the end of the block. I could see the walls and roof of the small structure tilting to the far left. Jagged shards of broken glass shone on the black sidewalk like scattered diamonds. The bus was there. It was also crashed into the side of the bus stop.

I slowed to a walk and moved around the side of the bus. The twisted remains of the bus stop blocked the front door. Steam from the broken radiator gushed from the front of the bus and obscured the view. It didn't look like anyone was inside. I didn't see the driver or any of the passengers, not even the homeless guy. They could have left after the crash. Maybe the ash blocked the driver's view and caused the accident? For some reason, I felt the urge to look inside.

Bodies lined the floor. I could see the driver and a few of the passengers sprawled out towards the front of the bus. The homeless guy was still missing.

Using my sleeve to wipe away some of the ash on the window, I pressed my face closer. A loud *thump* caused me to jump back and trip over some of the wrecked bus stop.

The homeless guy beat two bloodied fists against the window. His eyes were glassy and red. Strings of chunky vomit clung to his scraggly beard and danced lightly as he screamed at me from inside the bus.

"Go to the back door," I said through my sweatshirt. I pointed to the rear of the bus. "Go there."

I watched the homeless man shuffle to the back door. He stumbled and fell a few times and struggled to pull himself up from the floor. His bloody hands slipped on the plastic seats, but he continued forward. The short distance to the rear door seemed like an impossible task. He eventually got to the doors.

Standing at the bottom of the stairs, I waved for the homeless guy to hurry up. I didn't want to leave him on the bus if he was hurt, but I didn't want to stand around in the ash and slop either. He teetered at the top of the stairs and then pitched forward, slamming his head against the double doors. A patch of hair caught between the rubber that lined both doors.

"Holy shit," I said and pushed my fingers between the doors to pry them open. The homeless guy groaned and tried to push himself up from the floor. The tangled knot of hair that was between the doors sloughed off as he stood up, exposing a large section of bloody scalp. He pawed at his head, pulling away more hair and scalp with each pass. I saw his fingers poking through the tips of his gloves and could see the skin looked bubbled and raw.

I yanked the doors open. The smell of vomit, urine and death spilled out of the bus. My eyes watered, even though I still had my sweatshirt tied in place.

"Get out of there," I said and waved. The homeless guy turned towards me. Blood ran from his eyes like tears. I could see it dripping from his ears and nose. He opened his mouth to mumble something. Maybe to ask for help? But all that came out was a thick stream of vomit. It splashed on the rubber floor of the bus and trickled down the stairs in a revolting waterfall.

The homeless guy collapsed, hitting his face on a nearby seat and then tumbled down the stairs. I moved to catch him, but only managed to slip a few ratty dreadlocks between my fingers. They pulled off and he continued onto the sidewalk. I gagged looking at the knotted lengths of hair in my hand. They ended in frayed bits of red skin and meat. Panic surged in my gut.

I rolled the homeless guy over to check him, but he was gone. Poking my head into the bus it looked like the other people had suffered similar deaths. Wads of hair and skin littered the floor. Greasy smears of blood and skin streaked across the windows. I turned to run, not knowing what was going on, but knowing that I had to get as far from this bus as possible.

I had to leave. I had to get home. I had to see Lisa and Kara.

8

The ash stopped falling by the time I made it to my old neighborhood. The trees were coated in black and gray. The sun tried in vain to break through the clouds and succeeded in only casting a handful of sickly orange rays. I felt like I had never been set free this morning. I hated how the world looked almost as much as I just wanted to go home.

I don't know what I was expecting, but I was still surprised to see my house. After three years, it had become little more than a memory and the reality of putting my foot on the first step made me dizzy.

Closing my eyes, I could almost imagine Kara flying down the steps and into my arms. She would greet me every day I came home from work, everyday before I went to jail.

The truth was that I knew Lisa and Kara weren't going to greet me as I walked through the front door. Lisa and Kara left me before I went to prison, three years wasn't going to change that. It also didn't mean I wanted to see them again any less. Working menial jobs had left me with little money in the bank, but I had come into some money before prison and used it to set up a trust that kept my house out of foreclosure. I couldn't stand the idea of someone else living in my house. It was mine and the memories between those walls were priceless. I would have burned it to the ground before I let some stranger intrude on the place I remembered being the happiest.

A picture of Kara and Lisa hung in the front hallway. I never could bring myself to take it down. They had been so happy that day, we all had. It had been one of those impromptu weekend trips to nowhere and we had spent the day picnicking and hiking in the woods. I loved the way the sun framed the two of them in this picture. It looked like auras or halos. They never should have left. We should have stayed like that forever.

The house smelled stale. Motes of dust drifted in the air as I moved from one room to the next. The furniture was covered in plastic and bed sheets. I had done my best to close up the house before I went away. I wanted everything to be how it had been before everything fell apart. I knew it was stupid, but I guess I hoped that if I kept the house the same that Lisa and Kara would come back.

Knee-high drifts of ash blew along the wooden fence in my backyard. Seeing the black, powdery piles that had fallen from the sky shook me from memories of Lisa and Kara. I couldn't keep walking around with a sweatshirt wrapped around my face. I don't know what killed those people on the bus, but it had to have something to do with the ash.

My basement was cold and the air smelled damp. A large metal door was set into the far wall. Three locks were set into the door. I knew the combination to each by heart. The first lock was my birthday, then Lisa's and finally Kara's. I could have picked better combinations, ones that were harder to guess, but it felt right to use their birthdays. This bunker was where I kept things that would save our lives. Even though Lisa hated it, this was ours. I made this for my family.

I was alone. The door swung open and I looked at the three bunks set into the wall with a heavy heart. All the supplies had been designed to support three people. Everything I had ever done was for them.

A series of hooks hung from the wall near the door. Three NBC masks hung from the hooks. They looked a little strange, kind of like a fish bowl on my face, but they were designed to keep the wearer safe from nuclear, biological and chemical threats. I figured those three areas had to cover whatever was happening outside. I pulled my mask over my face and took a few deep breaths. It pressed on my face and the lens fogged a little. It was still better than the sweatshirt.

The two remaining masks hung on the wall. They were reminders of people who should be with me, people I was missing.

That shit that had fallen from the sky was still on my clothes. I stepped out of the bunker, undressed and put my clothes in a black trash bag. When I dropped my jeans to the floor, I heard the hollow *thunk* of my cell phone hitting the concrete floor. I dug it out of my pockets. I tied off the bag and then sealed it with duct tape. I cleaned up as best as I could and changed into a clean set of clothes from the supplies in the bunker. I would need to set up the decontamination shower later, but right now I was just too tired. After that, I grabbed a small, hard package that sat on the shelf. It was drab green and wrapped in plastic. I never could believe they fit these things in such a small bag.

I cut the plastic and removed the S-3 NBC suit from the plastic. It was a protective suit. The layers were lined with charcoal and should keep me safe. I pulled the drawstrings and sealed the cuffs. I didn't know what was outside, but this was my best bet at surviving it.

There was food on the shelves and bottled water, but I realized that my appetite had vanished. I would have to make sure to eat and drink something later. I walked past the shelves and further into the bunker, trying not to notice that everything was sectioned off in threes.

In the rear of the bunker, my guns hung on some pegs I had set into the wall. A thin coating of dust covered the weapons, but I had wrapped them in plastic after cleaning and oiling them. Knowing that I was going to get locked up allowed me enough time to make sure everything was squared away. A few minutes of cleaning and a little bit of new oil and the guns were good as new.

Near my gun rack was a HAM radio and a series of battery-powered chargers for cell phones and other electronic devices. I plugged my phone in and watched the screen blink to life.

I loaded my Mossberg 930 Special Purpose. As far as shotguns went, this was one of my favorites. A few extra shells were stuffed into my pockets. I don't know what I was getting ready for, but things were fucked up and I felt better holding a shotgun.

Someone screamed outside. It was angry. A second scream followed. It was a cry for help. I was halfway up the stairs before I realized I was moving.

Back in the bunker, a text message appeared on the small screen of my phone. I wouldn't see it until later, but its words would remain carved into my heart.

Kara: I miss you, Daddy. I love you.

9

A black dust devil raced across my front lawn. My eyes followed it. I couldn't see where the screams had come from. The streets were empty. At the end of my block, I could see a minivan crashed into the side of someone's house. A section of the roof had broken free and crushed the front half of the minivan. Was that where the yelling had been?

The woman screamed again. I could hear a man barking orders. It sounded like the noise was coming from my neighbor's house. I thought her name was Jane or something like that. She had a dog named Rusty or Fluffy or whatever. I think he was one of those pocketbook dogs. Of course, all that information meant nothing because in three years Jane could have moved and some new white trash couple could have moved in. Hell, maybe yelling at each other was their Friday night fun? Then I heard a child scream and start crying.

I racked a shell in my shotgun and cleared the steps of my neighbor's porch in one leap. Jane or not, I didn't care who was living next door to my house. There was a child in there.

The door was locked. It took three or four kicks to rip the bolt from the doorframe. Every Hollywood movie showed the police breaking doors down with one kick. I don't know if there was some special technique you learned at the academy, but I sure as hell didn't know it.

A woman was curled in a corner. It looked like she was trying to protect her son from the man that stood in the middle of living room. The boy was thrashing, trying to get out from behind his mother. He was foaming at the mouth. His eyes were wide with anger and his mouth was curled into a feral snarl. I didn't know who this man was or what he wanted, but the look on the boy's face told me more than I needed to know.

The man spun to face me, or more specifically, to face the business end of my Mossberg shotgun. His face was covered in boils. Some had burst, leaving raw sores wreathed with jagged, leathery skin. Clumps of hair had slipped from his scalp and were strewn about the carpet.

"Get. Out. Now." I motioned towards the door with my shotgun.

Blood zigzagged from the man's eyes. He squinted at me, as if trying to figure out what his next move was. I wasn't in the mood to wait and find out. The guy took a step towards me.

"Leave," I said and pulled the stock tighter against my shoulder. I was ready to kill this asshole if he left me no other choice.

"Get out, Ian," the woman shouted. She pointed towards the door with a trembling finger. I noticed that her skin looked normal, so did the boy's. Her words did nothing to calm the situation. Ian, whoever he was, turned and rushed the two people huddled in the corner.

The butt of my shotgun crashed into the back of Ian's neck. He let out a surprised yelp and fell to the floor. He lay there facedown, gurgling and pawing at the carpet. I pressed the barrel of my shotgun against his head.

"Run over to my house," I said. "It's the white one next door. Go down to the basement. I'll be right behind you."

"Next door?" the woman asked. "No one lives next door."

"I do," I answered. "Now go on over to my house."

The woman nodded and stood up from the floor. She used the wall to brace herself and I could see bruises on her arms. The boy had similar marks. My finger tightened around the trigger.

Once I heard the lady and boy run down the porch steps, I kicked Ian in the ribs as hard as I could. It was like driving my boots into a sack of laundry. His midsection lifted off the floor and thumped back down without so much as a grunt. I nudged him with the toe of my boot. He didn't move.

"Get up," I said. "Ian, get the fuck up." The NBC mask muffled my words, but he should have been able to hear my command. Ian remained still.

I placed my foot under his shoulder and pushed him over onto his back. The boils on Ian's face had burst and spilled yellowish-red pus across his face. His eyes were ringed in clotted lines of blood, but had clouded over and become dull and lifeless. Ian's chest and stomach were motionless. He was dead.

I left Ian on the living room floor.

-10-

My front door was open. The woman was in a rush. I could understand, but still, leaving the door open was a bad move. There could be more people like Ian or the homeless guy out there and the last thing I wanted was to invite them into my house. Still, I couldn't really blame her.

I walked into the basement and found the woman and boy standing near my bunker. They were staring into the interior and turned to face me as I came down the stairs. The boy stepped in front of the woman.

"Who are you?" the woman asked.

"My name is Lucas. This is my house. I was away for a while." I leaned my shotgun against the wall. They seemed harmless enough and I didn't want to scare them anymore than they already were.

"Thank you," the woman said. "I'm Danni and this is my son, Jared. We moved in next door a few months ago. Ian is my boyfriend."

"Was," I said.

"You killed him?" Danni asked. It was a simple question. There was no anger or sadness in her words.

"No, I didn't kill him," I answered. "Whatever the hell is going on out there killed him. I saw it kill some other people earlier today. I think it has something to do with the ash that fell from the sky."

"Why didn't it kill us?" Jared asked. He appeared to relax a little.

"Not really sure about that one," I said. "What I've seen looks a little like radiation poisoning, but there's something off about it. That should have affected everyone the same."

"Are you some kind of soldier or something?" Danni asked. "Were you deployed overseas?"

I laughed. "No, I was a construction worker. The stuff you saw inside my bunker was…um…well, I guess it was a hobby."

"Some hobby," Jared snorted. "So where were you?"

"Don't be rude," Danni said and slapped Jared's shoulder. A puff of ashy black dust rose into the air.

There was no reason to lie. I had nothing to gain from it and if these two didn't like what they heard, well then they could get the hell out. "I was in prison," I said.

"Prison?" Danni asked. "What did you do?" The question came a little too easy, perhaps practiced with other men in her life.

"I thought we weren't supposed to be rude," Jared said. "Besides, how many times did Ian go to prison? Who cares what Lucas did?"

"Manslaughter," I said. Again, honesty was just easier. "I served three years."

"Couldn't have been that serious if you only served three years," Jared said.

"Good behavior and overcrowding," I explained.

"Oh," Jared said. He stepped in front of his mother again.

"But it doesn't really matter, does it?" I asked. "I'm not telling you that you have to stay here with me. You're welcome to leave if you want."

"Leave?" Danni asked. "But what if we want to stay?"

"Then take you clothes off," I said. "Both of you."

"What?" Jared stepped towards me, his hands curled into fists.

I had been in prison too long and forgot that normal people explained things to each other. In prison, you just said what needed to be done or took it without talking. There was no time or reason to explain things to other inmates. They'd do what you said if they respected or feared you.

"Sorry." I held my hands up. "Your clothes are covered with ash. We need to bag them up in case it's toxic or radioactive. There are extra clothes inside the bunker. I'll go upstairs. Find something that fits. Put the dirty stuff into one of the black garbage bags and tape it up. Make sure you use the shower to clean off. Let me know when you're done."

I showed them where I had set up my decontamination shower in the far corner of the basement. It was near the dry well so the water would run in. It was a small portable, single person shower that I had order from Grainger. It cost more than my first car and at the time had seemed like something I'd never use. I was glad I had it.

Danni and Jared nodded as I showed them how the shower worked and where the trash bags and tape were. They looked scared. I couldn't really blame them.

I walked upstairs and collapsed onto the couch. A small puff of dust leapt off the sheet that covered it. Regular dust. I watched the motes waft around the room like an army of homeless fairies. I guess it was good that everything in the bunker had been in threes.

It should have been Lisa and Kara down there, not these strangers. She never should have left me.

I still missed my family.

Danni came up from the basement wearing some of Lisa's clothes. Jared had dressed in some of my old clothes. They were comically oversized. He had to roll the pants and sleeves. Kara's NBC suit should fit Jared. He looked to be about twelve or thirteen and bigger than Kara, but it should still fit. I was never sure when or if Kara would need it, so I bought a larger size. Lisa's suit would fit Danni fine.

I hadn't shown them the suits. They still stared at me like I was an alien, but the longer they spent walking around without a mask and suit, the more likely they would get sick or infected. Besides, I wasn't planning on staying here. They were welcome to do whatever they wanted, but I still needed to see my family again. That wasn't going to happen sitting around here.

"Come on," I said. I walked past Danni and towards the basement.

"Wait," Danni said. She stood in the doorway with Jared behind her. I turned to look at the two of them. "Can we eat something? Jared hasn't had anything to eat since this morning."

"The food is down here." I walked a few more steps, but didn't hear them following. "What is it?"

"Isn't the food in the kitchen?" Danni asked. She was a creature of habit, most people were.

"I wasn't here for three years, so there's no food in the kitchen," I said. "Besides that food would be contaminated. There's food in the bunker."

Danni and Jared followed me down the stairs. I stood at the door of the bunker.

"We're going to need to sleep in here tonight. There are beds and an air filtration system. We should be safe in here."

They hesitated. I couldn't really blame them. Some strange guy, who is admittedly an ex-con, busts down their door dressed like a damn space alien and then suggests that they lock themselves into his secret basement bunker. Yeah, I'd hesitate too.

"I'm not going to do anything," I said. "Don't you think I would have done it already? There's no lotion to put in baskets or any other Silence of the Lambs stuff. It's safe in here, that's all."

Danni nodded to Jared and then walked into the bunker. Jared looked into my mask as he walked past. I shrugged. There was no need to posture. This kid was protecting his mother. I got that.

Once they were inside, I walked across the basement and filled the generator with gas. Before I went away, I added stabilizer to my gas supply. I still wondered if it would hold up. The generator chugged to life and I checked the vent line to make sure we wouldn't kill ourselves with fumes, though I guess there were worse things that could happen. Everything looked in order. I switched the generator off. For now, we still had power from the grid so there was no point wasting the gas.

I walked into the bunker and closed the door. The lights set into the ceiling were on and Danni and Jared sat on two out of the three chairs inside. I twisted the handle to seal off the door and made sure the ventilation system was clear.

It felt good to take my NBC mask off. Sweat beaded on my face and could feel the indentation on the sides of my face where the mask created a seal. I grabbed a can of fruit cocktail from the shelf. There were other things to eat, but I remembered how much Kara loved the stuff. That was the only reason I had it in here.

"Fruit cocktail okay?" I set the can down on a nearby table and found the opener. Even though I was out of prison, the food looked about the same.

"Yeah, fruit cocktail is cool," Jared said. "Thanks, Lucas."

I spooned out three servings of the stuff and passed two to Danni and Jared. They nodded and began eating.

"We can sleep here tonight," I said between bites, "but tomorrow I'm leaving. I need to see my family."

"Your family?" Danni asked. "You have family out there?"

"Yeah," I said. "My wife, Lisa and my daughter, Kara."

"They don't live here with you?" Jared asked. His mouth was stuffed with fruit.

"No," I answered. "They left me before I went away."

"That happens," Danni said. "My parents split up when I was twelve. Sorry."

My phone sat on the table. Danni noticed as she looked around the room.

"Is that your cell phone?" Danni asked and walked towards the table it sat on. I snatched it off the table before she could reach the phone.

"Don't touch that," I said. Seeing the look on Danni's face, I added, "Uh, please? These things probably won't work much longer, if at all." I opened it and looked at the text message on the screen. Kara's simple words wound steel straps around my heart and twisted. I would tell her that I loved her soon.

"That looked like a text message," Jared said. He took his phone out of his pocket. "But I guess you're right. I don't have any bars on my phone, either."

I wanted to change the subject. "Once we know what's going on out there, we can figure out what our next move is."

"How are we going to do that?" Jared asked. "All the radio and television stations were nothing but static."

"Regular radios maybe," I agreed. I pointed towards a boxy HAM radio in the corner of the bunker. I had pieced this one together myself, swapping out parts and antenna to make it broadcast further.

"Does it work?" Danni asked.

"Let's find out." I walked over to the radio. Static crackled through the receiver. I checked a few channels. It was more of the same.

"Wait, go back." Jared rushed towards the radio. "There was something there. Go back. Go back."

Underneath the electronic fuzz, I could hear that Jared was right. There was a voice, maybe even more than one.

"Can you talk to them?" Danni asked.

"Not right now. I think the ash and storm are screwing with the signal," I said. "I've got an idea on how we can boost the signal tomorrow. Probably not a good idea try and fly a kite tonight."

"A kite?" Jared asked.

I would really need to work on the whole explaining things and people skills thing if I didn't want to sound crazy all the time. Or at least for whatever time was left.

-12-

Boxes of old toys and clothes were stacked in one corner of the basement. I hate clutter, but could never bring myself to throw away any of Kara's things.

"There should be a kite in that box." I pointed to the box labeled 'TOYS.' Jared began searching through it. Both he and Danni had put on NBC masks and suits. I still couldn't be sure what was going on outside, but wanted to be safe. I remembered something coming through the bus radio about an attack on cities, but found it hard to believe that any terrorist group could pull off something like this. Maybe a volcano had erupted or maybe Yellowstone finally blew? Those seemed more plausible than a terrorist attack. But with no TV or radio, we had no real information and any guess could be true.

"So what are you going to do with this, Ben Franklin?" Jared asked as he handed me the kite. I could see him smiling behind his NBC mask. He was a good kid.

I began putting the kite together. "Go get that thin spool of wire from the work bench over there."

"You're not really going to try and catch a lightning bolt, are you?" Jared handed me the wire.

"No," I laughed. It had been a while since I heard the sound of my own laughter and it sounded clumsy and out of practice. There wasn't much to laugh about in prison, unless of course you were a psychopath, in which case prison was hilarious. "That signal we picked up last night was weak. We need to find a way to boost our range. My HAM radio antenna is on the roof and I'd guess that all the ash that's in the air is screwing up the signal. This might help us get a better one."

"You're going to tie the wire to the antenna and try to fly the kite above some of the ash?" Jared studied the kite. "That's a good idea."

The kid was smart, too. That's probably how he managed to survive the string of losers that his mother brought home. I couldn't blame Danni. Hell, I was a loser too, but I never would have hit Lisa or Kara.

"Danni, you ready to go?" I asked. She walked out of the bunker. "You're going to need to hold the ladder. Jared, you go about halfway up and feed me the wire as I let the kite out."

"I'm as ready as I'm ever gonna be." Danni started up the stairs. I had offered to let her take one of my guns, something easy to use, like a .45, but she refused. Guns scared her. Besides, she had argued, everyone outside was dead, so what was the point of a gun? Jared volunteered to carry one. Danni looked like she wanted to kill him. I promised him I'd show him how to use one later.

Outside of my house was silent. There was a light wind blowing ash down the street like ragged black ghosts, but I didn't see any other people. They could have been holed up in their houses. They were probably dead.

"There's an extension ladder around the back," I said and walked off the porch. Small clouds of ash puffed underneath my boots with each step. I found myself wishing for rain to wash away some of the crap that choked my yard and street.

My ladder was underneath the back porch. Jared helped me pull it out and lean it against the gutters on the second story. I never was a fan of heights, but figured there were worse things to worry about these days. Danni held the bottom of the ladder as Jared and I climbed up.

"Wait here," I said to Jared when he was a little more than halfway up. I didn't want the kid to slip. "Feed me the wire as I let the kite out, okay?" Jared nodded.

Ash covered the roof of my house. It looked like Christmas in Hell. At any moment, I expected to see Satan flying by in a sled with skeletal reindeer and flames. He was evidently busy somewhere else. I was alone on the roof.

The HAM radio antenna was bolted to the side of my house at the highest point of the roof. I made my way to the top and sat with one leg on each side of the roof. The wind felt stronger up here, but it could have just been my fear and imagination getting the better of me.

I held the kite up and tested it against the wind. The fabric bowed and puffed out. It looked like it would fly.

"You ready?" I asked Jared. He gave me a thumbs up from where he stood on the ladder.

I angled the kite and let it go, feeding the thin wire through my hands. It climbed higher and higher. Jared continued to feed out the wire. I squinted, trying to keep the kite in view.

"Hold up," I said to Jared. I felt the wire go taut in my hands. I reached to my belt and withdrew my Leatherman from its sheath. Flicking my wrist, I opened the pliers. After the wire had been wound around the antenna, I cinched the wire with the pliers. A few belt clamps completed the job after I tightened them around the antenna with the flathead screwdriver. I checked the wire again. It looked like it would hold. It would have to, there were no more kites in the basement.

"Is it all set?" Jared asked as I shimmed down to the ladder.

"We're good," I said. "Now let's go check the radio before we lose our chance."

I was almost to the bottom of the ladder when I heard Danni cry out. Jared leapt the last few rung and landed on the ground in a black cloud of ash. I was close behind.

Ian, or what had once been Ian, stood in my backyard. A leathery corpse, clad in Ian's clothes, shuffled towards Danni. Its hair was gone and eyes a dull, dusty gray, but it definitely had been Ian. She held my shotgun I left it near the ladder. Now it was in her trembling hands. The barrel danced all over the place. There was no way she would be able to get a clean shot off.

"Ian?" Danni asked. Her words sound weak and distorted through the mask. She looked frozen.

"Mom," Jared yelled and ran to his mother's side. "Come on." He tugged at the sleeve of Danni's NBC suit. Danni didn't move.

I got there just as Ian lunged for Danni. His fingers were little more than bone wrapped in hardened, yellow skin. The boils on his face had burst and dried into black rings with jagged points of skin surrounding them. Images of that ice mummy some scientists had found flashed through my head.

I swung my arm, smashing it into Ian's neck. He stumbled back a few steps and then dove for my extended arm. I felt a strong squeeze on the sleeve and realized Ian was biting my arm. The thick fabric and layer of charcoal lining in my NBC suit kept him from getting through, but it still hurt like hell.

"Give me the gun," I said as I reached with my free hand. Jared grabbed it from Danni and passed it to me. I drove the stock into Ian's face and felt his nose crunch beneath it. He stumbled backwards and fell to the ground with his legs splayed out like a giant toddler.

I aimed the barrel in Ian's face. "Get the fuck out of my yard." He showed no recognition of the threat or command and scuttled forward on all fours.

Jared leapt past me and dropped onto the middle of Ian's back with both feet. I heard a dull snap and Ian's legs stopped moving.

We all watched, stunned and silent, as Ian continued to crawl across the yard. He showed no reaction to the damage or pain that had just be inflicted. His yellowed teeth chattered and clacked as he pulled himself forward.

"Shoot him." Jared pointed at Ian. "Shoot him."

I didn't hesitate. Ian's head exploded in a cloud of black and red. Bits of him splashed across my dusty yard, getting lost in the drifts of ash.

"I thought you said Ian was dead?" Danni asked, waking from her stupor.

"I checked him," I said. "He was dead."

"He is now," Jared snorted and toed the headless corpse with his boot. A thick black gel oozed from the ragged stump that had once been Ian's neck, but there was no blood.

"Let's get inside," I said and racked another shell into my shotgun. I had a feeling I was going to need it.

-13-

After rinsing off in the decontamination shower, I hung my suit and went to check the radio. Jared and Danni joined me soon after.

"Is your arm okay?" Danni asked. A large purple bruise in the shape of Ian's mouth blossomed on my forearm.

"It hurts," I said, "but he didn't break the skin."

"What was wrong with him?" Danni asked. "He looked sick."

"Sick?" Jared laughed. "He wasn't sick, mom, he was a fucking zombie."

"Don't curse," Danni said.

"Sorry," Jared shrugged, "but that doesn't change the fact that Ian was a zombie. What else would you call him? Lucas said he was dead and then Ian shows up and tries to bite a chunk out of his arm. Sure sounds like a zombie to me."

"You've been playing too many video games," Danni said. She turned towards me. "What do you think Lucas?"

"No idea," I said honestly. "Ian was dead. I'm sure of that. But that thing outside *was* Ian or at least had been."

"But do you really think he was a zombie?" Danni asked.

"Shit," I said. "I hope not." I looked at my arm, remembering all of the zombie movies I had seen.

"You're fine," Jared said, examining my arm. "He didn't break the skin, so you're cool."

"Thanks," I said and turned back to the radio.

Static popped and crackled on most channels. I had written down the channel we heard talking on the previous night. Now it was only white noise.

"Keep looking," Jared said. "Someone is out there. They have to be." I scrolled through a few more channels. I still couldn't make sense out of what Ian had become. He looked dried out and hardened, almost mummified. He most definitely looked dead, but could he really have been a zombie? I thought shit like that only existed in movies and videogames, but I couldn't argue with Jared's rationale. For lack of a better definition, Ian was a zombie.

"...*little more than husks of who they were...entire East and West Coasts...*"

The voice rattled through the radio. Everyone inside the bunker held their breath. My hand trembled, as if moving it might lose the voice. We were desperate for information.

"Can you talk to them?" Danni said. Her voice was barely above a whisper. I nodded.

"Please repeat," I said.

"*Who is this? What's your location?*" the voice asked.

"My name is Lucas," I said. "I'm on the East Coast. Where are you?" I wasn't going to tell them too much too soon. Disasters made people dangerous.

"*We're in Buffalo. Wait, did you say East Coast? Holy shit, Lucas,*" the voice said. "*How are you still alive?*"

"What do you mean?" I asked. "I've been holed up for over a day in my basement."

"*The entire East Coast is gone, so is the West,*" the voice said. "*Some kind of coordinated terrorist attack. They set off multiple dirty bombs around major cities. You've seen the ash falling, right?*"

"Yeah," I said. "But I didn't think dirty bombs would be capable of everything that I've seen outside. I'd expect some fallout and radiation poisoning, but nothing like what we've seen."

"You've seen the husks, haven't you?" the voice said. *"A handful of survivors are out there and they're all reporting husks in their towns and cities."*

"What the hell is a husk?" I asked. I was pretty sure that I already knew the answer.

"The dead," the voice said. *"Those bombs weren't just radioactive. They loaded them up with a myriad of viruses. Something happened when the bombs exploded, some kind of radioactive virus or something. Anyone who breathes in too much of the ash dies, but they don't stay that way. The radiation kills them and dries them out, but the virus brings them back. They come back as withered human husks. Then they eat. Have you or anyone you're with been bit?"*

I looked at the bruise on my arm. It had spread and yellowed on the edges, but it didn't look like anything more than a bruise.

"No," I said. "No one has been bit by one of those things. One tried, but didn't break the skin."

"That's good, that's very good, Lucas," the voice said. *"That's how the virus spreads."*

"He's talking about zombies," Jared said. "See I told you Ian was a fucking zombie."

"Jared!" Danni snapped.

I shrugged. The kid sounded pretty spot on.

"Are you saying people are coming back as zombies?" I asked into the radio. "That seems a little crazy."

"You must have seen one or two by now, Lucas," the voice said. *"People have been calling them 'husks' because I guess that's easier to wrap your head around. But, call them whatever you want, you're dealing with zombies."*

"So how are you in Buffalo?" I asked. "You said the East Coast was gone. Is that part of New York safe?"

"New York?" the voice said. I heard a garbbled laugh under the static. *"New York is a wasteland. I'm in Buffalo, South Dakota. There's a group of us that have joined up. The ash clouds haven't gotten this far. We're hoping that the Rocky Mountains will keep it on the West Coast and that everything in the East won't make it this far. Look, Lucas, I have no idea how you're still alive, but you need to get as far away from the East Coast as fast as possible. Maybe try and head this way. You're obviously a resourceful man. The world is going to need people like you."*

Whoever was on the other end of this radio spoke like it was his job. The words came too easy. In prison, I learned not to trust someone who always knew the right thing to say. There were only two types of people that spoke with that level of confidence – con men and politicians. Not that there was much of a difference between the two. I hated them both.

"We should go," Danni said. She stood up and paced the length of the bunker.

"Leave?" I asked. "We don't know who is on the other end of this transmission. Could be a bunch of psychos, or worse, liars. They might be worse off than we are."

Danni looked upset, but didn't argue.

I turned back to the radio. "How do we know we can trust you?"

"Lucas, I know you have no reason to trust or believe what I'm telling you, but there's going to be more husks with each day that passes," the voice said. *"Come here or don't, it's your call, but you need to get away from the East Coast."*

"I don't even know your name," I said. "Why am I going to suddenly pack up and leave?"

"My name is Senator James Heathway. I think I'm all that's left of the US Government," Heathway paused. *"You need to leave soon, Lucas. I hope you make the right choice."*

"Senator Heathway?" Jared asked. "I did a report about him for my social studies class, some kind of current events thing about

Second Amendment rights or something like that. I remember that he was from South Dakota. Maybe it really is him?"

"Yeah," I said. "Maybe it is, but that doesn't mean much."

"Doesn't mean much?" Danni asked. "He said he's what's left of the government. If we have any chance of surviving this, I'd say it's in South Dakota. I vote we leave."

"Me too," Jared said.

I hesitated. "I'm not making any snap decisions just because someone who may or may not be a US Senator told me to. Besides, I'm not going anywhere until I see my family."

"Your family?" Danni asked. I could see that she was conflicted. She would never tell me to give up on seeing my family, but she couldn't pass up the only chance that she might have to save hers.

"Okay," I sighed. "But you can't leave yet."

"Don't you mean *we*?" Jared asked.

"No," I said. "Look, I'll give you supplies, guns, and a map. I'll even help you find a better car than that pile of crap I saw in your driveway, but I'm not going with you. I'm sorry, but I just can't."

"Yes, you can," Danni said. She knelt down and looked into my eyes. "You don't even know where they are. Lucas, you can't pass up your only chance to go chase some memories. And even if you do find them, it might be worse than not knowing."

"Mom, that's not cool," Jared said. "Chill out about Lucas' family. I'm sure they're fine. I'm sure he had them just as prepared."

"I know where Lisa and Kara are," I said. I stood up and walked to the other end of the bunker. "I'm staying. You're going. That's the deal."

"What's first?" Danni asked.

"First?" I repeated. "First we get something to eat and then we get some rest. We'll start in the morning."

"Should we wait that long?" Danni asked. "Senator Heathway said we should leave as soon as possible."

"He also said that there were going to be more of those things like Ian, more husks," I said. "Do you want to go outside in the dark to find out if he's right? I don't." I grabbed a can from the shelf without looking at its label and began opening it. I wanted to do anything other than continue this conversation.

Danni shook her head. She was upset, but being impulsive would get someone killed. I would help her and Jared, make sure they were safe, but I wasn't going with them. I was going to see my family.

-15-

I listened to the sound of Danni and Jared snoring softly. Once I was sure they were asleep, I fished my cell phone out of my front pocket.

Kara: I miss you, Daddy. I love you.

I thumbed the keys on my cell phone, but nothing happened. The keys must have been broken as I was thrown to the ground and arrested. I wanted to write something back to Kara. I wanted to tell her that I loved her too, to tell her that I even still loved her mom. I wanted to be where they were, to make sure that they were safe.

Tears stung my eyes as I read Kara's text message for a second and then a third time. She was my little girl and I wanted to tell her that I loved her, but my shitty phone was broken. Lisa thought it was funny to tease me about still having a flip phone. She and Kara had smart phones. I resisted, claiming that those phones gave away too much personal information, but I would have traded anything for a phone that could reach Kara. But who knows? Even if I had been able to send it, it wouldn't have made the situation any better. She was still there and I was still here.

Kara: I miss you, Daddy. I love you.

I read the words again.

"I love you too, baby girl," I said. I knew she couldn't hear me, but prayed that she knew, that no matter where Lisa and Kara were, that they both knew that I loved them.

I would hug them and tell them that I loved them. I would do whatever I needed to do to see them again.

-16-

My old 1988 blue and white Ford Bronco II sat in the garage behind my house. Like most other things, I made sure to prepare it for the years I would be away. I drained the fluids and covered the truck. Still, I worried a squirrel or rat could have made a nest in the engine. It wouldn't be the first time I had seen one of the little bastards strip wires and stuff an engine with leaves and garbage.

I opened the door and popped the hood. Jared lifted it up. I breathed a sigh of relief when I saw no signs of rodents.

"We need to refill all the fluids," I said and pointed to varying cans and drums in the corner of the garage. "Drag those over here while I switch out the spark plugs and check a few other things."

Jared stopped near the open driver's side door.

"What is it?" I asked.

"No offense man, but this truck kind of sucks," Jared said. "I would have guessed that you had some bad ass Road Warrior thing in here."

"That Mad Max shit will get you killed," I said. "You don't want metal plates and saw blades. What you want is something with four-wheel drive that's easy to maintain and has a lot of parts available. And that's this ugly beast right here."

"Still, man, it looks like it handles like a fat kid on roller skates," Jared said.

"It does," I said. "But I know how to make it run and keep it running, so that's good enough for me." Jared smirked and walked towards the back of the garage.

Danni was inside collecting supplies for their trip. I didn't feel like I needed to watch her. There was more than enough stuff in my basement and I wasn't planning on going far, so whatever they needed to get to South Dakota was fine with me.

Jared struggled with the drum of gas. "Move it like this," I said and showed him how to tip it onto its edge and roll it. Once the barrel was in place, I grabbed the hand crank pump from the bench. Jared held the gas line in place while I cranked the pump. With the tank topped off, we began dealing with the oil and other fluids.

After a few turns of my ratchet, we had changed out the last of the spark plugs. A new battery was next. The Bronco II looked like it might actually run.

"Come on, kid, I'll show you how to start this up. I'm guessing you've never driven a car before," I said. I climbed into the driver's side.

Jared opened the passenger door and climbed in. "I've driven a car before, but never one with a stick shift."

"You're not old enough to have a license," I said as I pumped the pedal to prime the engine. The truck sputtered a few times and then kicked over. An acrid cloud of exhaust belched from the tail pipe and filled the garage with a hazy fog.

"I don't have a license," Jared said. "Believe it or not, the guy my mom was dating before Ian was worse. He beat her up so bad one night that I had to drive her to the hospital. I hit a few things, like some trash cans and a mailbox, but I got her there."

"Gotcha," I nodded. Jared had lived a short life, but a hard one. He might actually have a chance of surviving this insanity. He deserved it.

The Bronco II rumbled out of the garage and into the yard. Ian's headless corpse was somewhere beneath the mounds of ash that dotted my yard. I hoped we wouldn't run him over, but figured it didn't really matter.

Static roared from the radio. I must have forgotten to turn it off. Jared reached over and twisted the knob to silence the noise.

Danni shrieked from inside the house.

-17-

Danni fell down the stairs of my porch and crashed to the ground in an ashy cloud.

"Mom," Jared yelled and rushed forward. I grabbed his shoulder and pulled him back. "Let me go!"

"Stay here," I said. I wasn't going to argue with him and my tone let him know. Jared tensed, but stayed put.

The outline of a person swayed in the doorway of my house. It shuffled onto the porch.

Yellowed skin clung to the small frame of what looked to have once been an elderly woman. The ratty remains of a housecoat hung from her shoulders. It fluttered as she limped forward. The floral pattern of the dress turned black on her left side where a large wound had dried and clotted. The old woman's skin, already wrinkled, had hardened in leathery ridges that cut across her face like canyons. Her eyes stared without blinking and remained focused on Danni.

Danni scuttled across the front lawn on all fours like a crab. I stepped between her and the husk. Jared rushed to his mother.

"Jared, get your mother to the side of the house," I said. I backed away from the porch, leading the husk into the yard.

It stepped forward with no recognition of the stairs. I heard the bones in the woman's ankle snap as her foot rolled under her body. The husk tried to stand on its ruined ankle, but collapsed to the ground. Splintered white edges of bone jutted out from desiccated skin.

I led the husk into the middle of the yard. It reached for me with a thin, branch like hand. I aimed my shotgun at the husk's head and pulled the trigger. Its body twitched in the ash for a few seconds and then went still. There was no blood. Something clotted and spoiled splashed across my lawn, but there was no blood. There hadn't been any when I shot Ian and there wasn't any now. What Senator Heathway said must have been true. The radiation must be drying the husks out, even their blood.

"Lucas," Jared yelled. I turned to see him supporting Danni's body. She was curled forward and vomiting into the ash.

"Where the hell is her mask?" I asked as I helped Jared get Danni inside. It lay on the floor in my front hallway.

"It pulled it off," Danni said. Her voice was strained and strings of vomit dangled from her chin. "I should have looked before I opened the door. I thought it was you and Jared."

"Were you bit?" Jared asked. His words were thin and high. He tried to put Danni's mask over her face, but she vomited and he pulled it away.

"No," Danni said. "No, it didn't bite me."

"It's the ash," I said. "She must have breathed in too much."

"Is she going to become one of them?" Jared asked. "Lucas, do you think she's going to change into a husk."

"I don't know," I said. It was the truth. "But I don't think so. You're mom didn't have her mask off for too long. She's showing a few signs of radiation poisoning. We need to get her downstairs and into the bunker."

We helped Danni into one of the bunks. She was sweating, but the vomiting had stopped for the time being.

"What are we going to do?" Jared asked.

I rushed over to the red medicine cabinet that hung on one of the walls. I grabbed a small orange bottle with an eyedropper in the cap. "Give her a few of these drops ever hour until I get back." I passed a bottle of white pills to Jared next. "Give her three of these every four hours."

"Get back?" Jared said. He took the bottle with shaky hands. "What is this? Where are you going?"

"The eye dropper is potassium iodide," I said. "It'll help with the radiation poisoning, but I don't think it's strong enough. I'll need to go to the pharmacy and find something stronger. The pills are antibiotics. I'm hoping they'll wipe out any infection and bring your mom's fever down. If I can find something better in the pharmacy, I'll grab it, but these are pretty strong. She's going to be okay." I don't know if I said the last part to myself or to Jared, probably both.

"Lucas, it's getting dark," Jared said. "What about the husks?"

I walked to the back of the bunker and took a Smith & Wesson M&P 9mm handgun down from where it hung next to the other weapons. I bought this gun for Kara. It was light and had little to no kickback. Jared should be able to handle it fine.

"You've got one shot in the chamber and seventeen in the magazine," I said. "How many shots is that total?"

"Eighteen," Jared said.

"Good," I said. "Eighteen is all you've got. I don't have time to go over everything about shooting with you. The safety is off so don't screw around with the gun. If you need to use this, just point and squeeze the trigger. Don't pull the trigger. Just squeeze it lightly. You got it?"

"Yes," Jared said. He looked over to his mother.

"Jared, listen to me," I said. "I'm going to leave the gun on the table. Don't pick it up unless you need to use it."

"Okay, I won't," Jared nodded.

"But if you need to use it, don't hesitate," I said.

"No husks are going to get down here," Jared said.

"Jared, listen to me," I said. My voice was sharp and startled the kid. "You see any husk, no matter who they used to be, and you shoot it. Don't hesitate. They aren't people anymore, got it?"

Jared cast a quick glance to where his mother lay on the cot. He couldn't bring himself to say yes, but nodded. I hoped he wouldn't need to use the gun, but didn't want to leave him without one.

"I'll be back as soon as I can," I said and pulled my mask down. "Now repeat everything I just told you."

"One shot in the chamber and seventeen in the magazine for a total of eighteen shots," Jared said. He looked at the handgun. "I squeeze the trigger. Don't pull it. And I don't hesitate, no matter who the husk used to be. I got it."

I squeezed his shoulder. "Good. Be safe kid. I'll get back as fast as I can. Make sure to look after your mom, okay?"

Jared had tears glistening in his eyes, but nodded. He knew what that meant. He understood why the gun was on the table.

-18-

The pharmacy was three blocks from my house. I thought about taking the Bronco II, but decided against it. We needed to save gas and I didn't want to risk getting the truck stuck somewhere. Besides, going on foot would give me a chance to scout the streets and find the best route for Danni and Jared to leave.

A tangled knot of cars choked the intersection at the end of my street. I could see a few mangled bodies in the cars. I aimed the shotgun at the motionless corpses. They still had some hair and didn't look as desiccated as the husks, but I wasn't taking any chances. They didn't move. The crash must have killed them. I filed that information away. I was desperate to grasp whatever understanding of this situation was available, even small bits of information.

The rain had stopped a day ago. When it first started, I was angry and cursed the clouds as I ran down the sidewalk, but in retrospect, the rain must have saved my life. The ash being wet and stuck to the ground is what kept me alive, not my childish attempt to protect myself with a sweatshirt held over my face.

Now, as the ash began to dry out and once again become airborne, my NBC mask would keep me safe. Danni had her mask knocked off while fighting with the husk and I saw how that turned out. Hopefully she hadn't taken too much of that crap into her lungs. I shuddered thinking about what Jared would have to do if she had. I reached back and tightened the straps on my mask.

I turned left on Davidson Avenue and headed towards the pharmacy. This was a journey I had made more times than I could remember. Kara's birth transformed Lisa and me from rational human beings into hypochondriacs that panicked at the sound of our daughter's slightest sneeze. The pharmacy was open twenty-four hours and I could remember the look of fear in all the other fathers' faces as we sorted through the boxes of medication at 1AM.

When I held Kara on the day she was born, I made her countless promises. I was her father and that meant more than I could possibly comprehend while standing in the delivery room. Lisa fought through thirty hours of labor to bring our baby girl into this world. I loved her before Kara arrived, but after seeing the pain and work she went through to give me a daughter, she was a goddess. Lisa lay on the delivery bed exhausted and slick with sweat. She had never looked more beautiful. I had never loved her more. I pushed these memories out of my head.

A group of five or six husks shuffled towards me from the end of Davidson. They were slow, but I wasn't going to wait around for them to get closer. I had a good deal of rounds stored in my bunker, but it wasn't unlimited. I had to save it whenever I could.

I ducked between two buildings. I think one was a bank and the other was empty. It had been an ice cream parlor at one point. I remembered sitting at the little bar inside with Kara and buying her first milk shake. Her eyes were the size of saucers as she stared at the mountain of blended chocolate ice cream and heaps of whipped cream. She hardly noticed the cherry topping the thing off. A stomachache of monstrous proportions followed, which Lisa had been pretty pissed about. But I didn't care about Lisa's anger. That day had been wonderful, even a late night run to the pharmacy for Pepto couldn't change that. Everything could fall to shit, but none of that mattered if I had Lisa and Kara. I missed them.

A husk dove from behind a dumpster, forcing me against the brick wall. My mask grated against the rough brick and I worried that it might come loose. The clacking of the husk's teeth in my ear was deafening. From the corner of my eye, I could see ragged bits of flesh waving like tattered ribbons between the husk's teeth. Its painfully distended stomach pressed against me. It had just finished a meal and was hungry for seconds.

I waited for the husk to lunge forward and then dropped low, ramming my shoulder into the husk's chest, wrapping my arms around its bulbous gut. I felt rib bones grate against my shoulder as

I drove the thing across the alley. It clawed at my back and gnashed its teeth, but couldn't seem to get ahold of me. As we hit the opposite wall, I stepped back and brought my elbow around in a tight downward arc. The husk's withered nose crunched and twisted beneath my elbow. It showed no reaction.

The husk loped forward, its arms outstretched and milky, spoiled eyes fixed on me. A chorus of dull groans echoed from the mouth of the alley. More husks shuffled in, cutting off the direction I had come down the alley.

The husk with the broken nose stumbled across the alley and dove forward in a clumsy attempt to knock me to the ground. Alone these things weren't much of a threat. I could easily knock them to the ground and shoot them or just out run them, but what they lacked in speed and intelligence, they more than made up for in numbers. I was going to be overwhelmed.

I stomped on the neck of the husk that had leapt for me. It wouldn't kill it, but would put it out of action long enough for me to escape. Stepping over the husk, I ran towards the dumpster and yanked it away from the wall. The wheels were coated with grease and clogged with garbage. They squealed in protest, but I was able to wrestle it into the middle of the alley. Leathery arms and boney fingers grabbed for me from the narrow space between the dumpster and the walls. For now, they were too weak to get past the giant metal box of garbage. Soon, enough husks would be there to push it out of the way. I wasn't going to wait around to see.

The alley turned left. Streetlights had begun to flicker on, but shed no light between the buildings. I wondered how long the power grid would continue before it went black. Not much longer, I figured.

My path was clear. The alley ended on Palmer Street. The pharmacy was on the corner across the street. I pressed myself against the wall of the alley and tried to remain hidden in the shadows. Palmer looked empty. Maybe most of the husks had been drawn to Davidson by the sounds of the others.

I stepped out from the alley onto the sidewalk and jogged to a parked car. I squatted behind the car and surveyed the street. Most of the streets looked clear. When the ash began to fall, most people probably slowed or stopped their cars. They probably even got out to investigate. Humans were stupid like that. Danger could clearly be written on the side of something and we couldn't help but stick our hand inside. Our biological disregard of common sense had at least ensured that the streets were going to be easy to navigate.

Some cars had crashed into telephone poles or buildings, but I didn't think Danni and Jared would have a problem finding a clear route out of town. I edged around the parked car and looked up and down Palmer. Some shadowy forms stumbled around in the intersection at one end, but I could avoid them if I stayed quiet.

The right leg of my pants snagged on something underneath the parked car. A husk clung to my leg with its skeletal fingers. I kicked out, trying to knock the husk free. I missed. My boot *thunked* against the bumper of the parked car. The air in my lungs froze.

Please don't. Please don't. Please don't. I pleaded inside my head.

The headlights began to flash. The car alarm wailed. I heard a horn. The husks heard a dinner bell.

-19-

Husks came from all directions. They spilled from smashed storefronts like water from a burst dam. More shambled out of darkened alleys and stumbled into the street. I turned to try and find an avenue of escape, but the street was choked with the dead in both directions.

The car alarm continued to emit a banshee's wail, calling more husks from their hiding places. I thought about shooting the car's battery in an attempt to silence the stupid thing, but it wouldn't have made a difference at this point. The screech of the car alarm became a muffled din beneath the groans and growls of the husks.

I ran. I didn't know what else to do. Danni still needed medicine and I was too close to turn back and find another pharmacy. I sprinted across the street, my breath fogging the lens of my NBC mask.

My shotgun swept back and forth as I ran. A husk loped out from behind a liquor store. It wore the stained remains of a postal worker's uniform. The hat still clung to the husk's head, holding stringy clumps of hair in place. A shoe slipped from the husk's skeletal foot as it stepped off the curb and stumbled towards me. I turned and fired.

The shot tore the husk's gut open and spilled the dried remains of its intestines across the pavement. The husk spun in a morbid pirouette and collapsed to the ground. It struggled back to its feet. The jerky-like organs crunched beneath the husk's feet as it continued towards me. I could see desiccated flakes of skin and organs clinging to the blue postal uniform. They fluttered free with each stilted movement and were lost in the ash that littered the street. I racked another shell and aimed for the head.

Jared was right. I realized that I hadn't fully accepted his version of things until now. The husks were zombies. These weren't sick people. They weren't human. They had been at one time, but whatever was in the air and the ash had changed that.

Every zombie movie I had ever seen played through my head in fast-forward. I lined up the next shot for the husk's head. The postal worker's hat was thrown into the gutter as its owner's head disappeared. Greasy strands of hair fluttered like sea grass before being carried away by the breeze.

The husks were closing in. I still had a decent lead, but it wouldn't last. The minute I stopped running, they would catch up. The pharmacy stood on the corner.

The lights were still on inside of the pharmacy. No one had time to close stores before they became ill. I was glad to see the rows of neon bulbs emitting their sickly light, but that feeling quickly withered and died.

The doors were automatic, folding back on themselves when I stepped on the pressure pad. At one time, this had seemed convenient. Now it felt like a death sentence.

I was pretty sure that husks lacked the ability and intelligence to open a door, but this door would open itself for them. A second set of automatic doors waited behind the others.

The moment the opening was large enough, I squeezed through and sprinted for the aisle on the far side of the pharmacy. Boxes of light bulbs, clothespins and cheap tools hung from hooks in the home supplies aisle. I searched the bins beneath these things. There had to be something I could use to buy myself enough time.

I grabbed a spool of clothesline and a roll of duct tape. Sprinting back to the front of the pharmacy I saw the first husk stumble onto the pressure pad in front of the first set of doors. The doors folded outward, knocking the monster onto its ass. Two more husks tripped over their downed comrade.

Winding the clothesline between the security sensors and the handles on the inner doors, I closed them off as best as I could. I wound the entire roll of duct tape around the clothesline with the hopes that it would make it stronger.

The husks spilled through the first set of doors and flooded the small entryway. They tripped over each other and clawed at the doors. I watched greasy smears of gore appear behind their fingers like a snail's trail. The doors jerked and shook as they tried to open automatically. The security sensors wobbled. It wouldn't be long before they toppled and the doors opened. I needed to hurry up and find the fuse box to kill the power or find medicine for Danni and get the hell out of here.

The only question was how I was going to do that, now that husks surrounded the pharmacy.

-20-

In the back of the storeroom, I found the breaker and killed the power to the pharmacy. I didn't like the idea of searching the store in the dark, but killing the power kept the doors closed and bought me a little more time.

The inside of the pharmacy was a sea of shadows. The windows were set high in the wall and let through a limited amount of moonlight. The shelves towered over the sides of the aisle and cast them in deeper shades of black and purple. I hadn't seen any husks when I first entered the pharmacy and was pretty sure they would have come after me if they were inside, but I wasn't about to take any chances.

I moved down the cold medicine aisle towards the pharmacy counter in the rear of the store. It was a straight shot and I didn't see anything lurking in the shadows. As I got to the counter, I swept my shotgun over the other aisles. They were empty.

A set of saloon-style doors led behind the pharmacy counter. I used the barrel of my shotgun to push them open and couldn't stop the soundtrack of a cheesy spaghetti western from playing through my head. There were shelves near the front of the pharmacy area that held things like cold medicine and other over the counter drugs that now had to be monitored. When I was in prison, the guy in the cell next to mine was there for buying three counties worth of Sudafed. It was amazing what white trash could accomplish and still stay white trash. I guess meth was the new moonshine, but neither was doing much to lift anyone out of the trailer park.

I pushed a few boxes of things into my backpack. There were supplies in my basement, but a little extra Tylenol wouldn't hurt and could be used for bargaining with people. Once Jared and Danni left for South Dakota, they were going to need to be prepared for a world unlike any they had ever seen. Money doesn't mean shit if there are no banks and government to say that it still does. Something like a bottle of painkillers or cough medicine might end up being worth more than a whole stack of hundreds.

Searching over the shelves, I grabbed a few other boxes and bottles of medicine that I wouldn't have previously been able to obtain. We needed to be ready to be our own doctors from now on.

A white box of 130 mg potassium iodide tablets sat on the far shelf in the back. It wasn't something the pharmacy made regular use of, so it had been moved back here. The drops I left with Jared would hopefully keep things from getting worse, but they sure as hell weren't going to make it better. I threw the potassium iodide into my bag and followed it with a bottle of grape flavored Pedialyte. I remembered buying the stuff when Kara had a fever and the doctor told us she needed to keep hydrated. She hated the stuff, but unlike a toddler, reason could make Danni drink the foul-tasting liquid.

I moved around the counter and computers that loomed in the middle of the pharmacy area. My boot thumped against something soft. I looked down at the leg of a man in a white pharmacist jacket. He was slumped against the counter. An open bottle of Oxycodone had spilled across the floor near his left hand. His face was blue and slightly puffy. I was relieved to see that it wasn't dried out and leathery. The one thing about that husks that I guess might be considered helpful, was at least you could easily tell who was and wasn't one of them. Then again, I thought Ian was dead and he came back as a husk, so the same thing could easily happen here. I toed the corpse and the pharmacist slumped over onto the floor. That was good enough for now. I wasn't planning on staying long enough to find out.

The front doors groaned and I heard the sharp pop of plastic breaking. Husks spilled through the front doors of the pharmacy in one rotted mass. I leapt over the counter and ran.

-21-

The husks tripped over the ones that had fallen to the floor. The toppled security towers and broken doors provided a second set of obstacles, but there was no stopping the husks. They were single minded in their focus. All they could see and understand was that I was somewhere inside the pharmacy and that I could be eaten. I think it was the second part that drove them. The husks appeared to have no real motivation beyond eating. They showed no fear of fire or weapons. All they wanted was to feed.

I sprinted towards the left side of the pharmacy. The storeroom had a rear exit that should open on the far side of the building. The noise and other husks should draw any of the ones outside to the inside and hopefully there wouldn't be any waiting for me.

The inside of the storeroom had no windows. Piles of boxes towered around me like long-forgotten obsidian obelisks. I tried not to imagine countless husks hiding behind each box, but my imagination had turned against me. In the shadows, I saw teeth gnashing and skeletal fingers ready to tear into my flesh.

I could hear the husks toppling shelves and groaning as they made their way towards the storeroom. I pushed the bar to open the back door. A fire alarm began to wail. The small red box set above the handle beeped incessantly, calling out to any nearby husks. The power was off, but the alarm continued. It must have some sort of back-up battery. I thought about shooting the alarm. It was more out of anger than anything else. The husks would have already heard the sound and were no doubt stumbling towards it. A blast from my shotgun was only going to make more noise and leave me with one less shell.

I ran out into an alley behind the pharmacy and slammed the door. I could still hear the alarm droning inside the pharmacy. The husks inside were going to be drawn to it and eventually they would push against the door and get it open. A wooden fence cut off the far end of the alley, so I turned and headed back towards the street.

Husks stumbled through the streets in giant knots of leathery flesh. They were preserved, almost jerky-like. Any time I had engaged in the zombie apocalypse debate with friends, I would argue that all you had to do was wait for them to rot away. Weather, bugs and decay were all on our side. I was wrong. The husks were desiccated, completely dried out and persevered. They weren't ever going to rot. I was sure they would wear down, maybe fall apart from walking endlessly, but they weren't going to decay.

More of the disgusting creatures fell through open doors and shattered storefronts. Most were following the sound of their dead comrades and the wail of the fire alarm to the front of the pharmacy. This was perhaps my best and only chance to escape.

I moved out from the alley. The streetlights had flickered on, painting the ash-choked streets in orange and gray. I seemed incapable of escaping the two colors that I hated the most. I ducked behind a pickup truck that was parked near the curb.

A husk lunged from behind a nearby mailbox. Its skeletal fingers raked across my NBC suit as it tried to pull me to the sidewalk. I stomped on its neck and felt the reverberation of vertebrae snapping. Its mouth continued to work and its dusty, gray eyes spun wildly in deep boney sockets as the husk still tried to bite me. My boot crushed the side of the husk's skull, releasing a thick black gel that oozed across the sidewalk and dribbled into the street. The husk was dead, or at least dead again, but the lack of blood was still unsettling. I had seen plenty of blood in prison, some of it my own, and never enjoyed the sight of it. But the utter lack of it in the husks spoke to a lost degree of humanity that my mind wasn't ready to deal with.

More husks had turned towards me. They stumbled across the street. The sound of their clumsy, stilted steps and moans drew more husks from the front of the pharmacy. A small mob turned the corner and loped towards me.

I turned and ran back for the alley. The husks followed, but I reached the high wooden fence before they could catch me. Enough of them would fill the alley and topple the fence, but not before I was long gone.

Straddling the fence, I turned back to look at the husks. I knew I should be running, but couldn't stop myself from staring at the monsters. These had been people I passed on the street, people I might have called friends. What looked to have once been a woman stumbled down the alley. Her leathery skin scraped against the brick side of the pharmacy. A patch of skin peeled away, revealing her elbow bone, and fluttered to the ground. She showed no reaction.

Watching the husks from atop the fence flooded me with an odd anger. I wanted to kill them. I wasn't sure if it was their lack of humanity or the loss of it that angered me. Was I mad that they were monsters or that they had been forced to become them?

My phone beeped. Another text message came through. I had no service. How were these texts getting through?

Kara: Daddy, where are you? I miss you.

The anger bled out of my body. My heart twisted and hurt.

The stupid buttons wouldn't light up. They were broken. I couldn't send a message back.

"I'm coming, Kara," I said, barely above a whisper, and leapt over the other side of the fence.

-22-

I managed to avoid most of the husks as I made my way back towards my house. Two or three husks stumbled into my path. These husks came at me one at a time. If it had been a collective effort, I would have been left with no other choice but to shoot them. Saving ammo and making as little noise as possible were two of my main goals besides staying alive. I smashed their skulls with the stock of my shotgun and splashed their rotted insides across the pavement.

Thick, gloppy chunks clung to the ashy pavement like some long-forgotten primordial slime mold. I stepped over the mess, not wanting to track any into the bunker and honestly just being disgusted by it.

The streetlights still provided sepia pools of light, but I clung to the shadows that grew between houses. From what I had seen, the husks weren't capable of hiding or setting a trap. They wandered through the streets, until something caught their attention and then they attacked. The only motivation or thought the husks appeared to have was to feed. That knowledge was unsettling, but also helped me avoid the husks. As long as I was quiet and didn't appear to be a meal, other things would distract the husks.

I turned the corner to my block. The world was painted in shadows. Objects, covered in ash, had soft edges and looked blurry in the limited illumination of the streetlamps. My house was towards the middle of the block. I could have found my way home blindfolded, but saw that wouldn't have been necessary.

A set of blinding headlights lit up the front of my house. A boxy black Hummer was parked diagonally on my lawn. A row of extra lights on the roof of the SUV painted my house in white. A few husks stumbled towards my steps, attracted to the noise that trickled out from the open front door. More would be there soon.

Someone had collapsed on the stairs of my porch. The husks shuffled past the body. If there had been even the slightest flicker of life left in it, the husks would have torn the body apart.

I moved around the edge of Danni's house and ducked down behind her parked car. The silhouette of a person moved in the driver's seat of the Hummer. From the size and outline, it appeared to be a man. He didn't look too concerned about the husks. Whoever these assholes were, I knew why they were in my house. They were looters. I don't think they knew about my supplies, but they probably stumbled across my house after going through a few others. I'm sure if Jared put up a fight or they found the bunker, either one would give them reason enough to stay. I hoped that Jared had been smart enough to seal the bunker and stay put.

The driver of the Hummer waited for the husks to stumble up the stairs before he opened the door and leapt out of the stupidly oversized vehicle. He wore a cheap respirator – the type used for painting, and carried a rifle. It looked like a deer rifle or something of that nature.

At first, I worried that these guys were cut from the paramilitary psycho cloth. The kind that spent their entire lives hoping and preparing for a disaster like this. Granted, I spent my time preparing, but I wasn't happy to be right. I wanted nothing more than to be wrong. These guys were the type that saw a disaster as a chance to lose their humanity and prey upon other people. That wasn't me. I just wanted to keep my family safe. And now, these assholes were preventing me from helping Danni and going to see Lisa and Kara. That was something I couldn't allow.

The driver shouldered his rifle and shot the first husk in the back of the head. Chunky splotches of black, red and gray splattered across the front of my house and trickled to the porch. The other husks, having heard the shot, turned towards a closer meal. The driver chambered another round and shot a second husk and then a third. He may have had a stupid car and cheap respirator, but he was good shot. I would need to be careful.

The last husk tripped from two steps above and crashed to the sidewalk below my porch. I could hear the muffled laughs of the driver from beneath his mask. He pulled the strap of his rifle over his shoulder and knelt on husk's back. Pulling a large hunting knife from the sheath on his belt, the driver began carving long lines into the husk's face. After a few more lines, the driver used the tip of his knife to peel back the hardened skin. The husk thrashed beneath him, not because it was in pain, but because it was hungry.

I'm not sure why, but watching this guy abuse the husk filled me with rage. I hated the husks. I hated what they were, but I was still sad that they had lost who they once were. Killing a husk was something I would never lose sleep over, but I did it because I had to, not because I thought it was fun.

The driver was busy skinning the husk and blind to the fact that I had crept up behind him. I whistled.

The driver turned, a stunned look in his eyes. I smashed the butt end of my shotgun into his face. His nose exploded beneath his respirator. Blood dribbled out the chin of his mask. I grabbed the side of his head and pushed him forward.

The husk beneath the driver's knees lunged forward and buried its teeth into the nearest soft target – the driver's crotch. He let out a muffled scream and tried to stand, but the husk had clamped onto his crotch and shook its leathery neck like I had seen alligators do on a nature show I used to watch in prison. The driver dropped his hunting knife and beat at the husk with his fists. It held strong.

Arms flailed and tried to grab the rifle on his back, but the driver couldn't reach it. I let the husk tear a wet chunk free and begin chewing. It thudded back to ground in a cloud of ash and blood. The driver was too stunned to scream. His eyes, wild with pain, alternated from staring at his ruined crotch, the chewing husk and the stranger standing behind him.

I picked up the driver's hunting knife. He stumbled towards me, his hands cradling the ruined remains of his crotch. Blood spurted from between his fingers and dotted the ashy ground below. I grabbed a fistful of his hair and yanked his head sideways. The hair slid off his scalp in a greasy tangle. I gagged and tossed it aside. Whatever masks these guys were wearing, it only appeared to be slowing down their deaths. I plunged the hunting knife into the driver's neck, twisted it and pulled it sideways.

Pulling the hunting knife free, I let the driver's body fall to the ground. The husk scuttled through the ash and buried its face in the open wound. It yanked a stringy wad of meat free and began chewing. I drove the hunting knife into the back of the husk's skull. It collapsed onto top of the driver. I wrenched the blade free, cleaned it off on the driver's clothes and slid it through my belt.

I made my way up the front steps of my porch and into the front of the house. Stopping to listen, I could hear men shouting in the basement. I didn't hear Jared or Danni.

Moving to the top of the basement stairs, I expected a fight. The stairs were empty. Whoever was in my basement, they were preoccupied with something else and weren't expecting anyone else to come home.

"Smart kid," I muttered. Jared must have heard the men coming through the front door and locked the bunker. I racked a shell in my shotgun and crept down into the basement.

These assholes were keeping me from seeing me family. They were going to regret that.

-23-

"Come on, kid, just open the damn door," one of the three men in my basement said. "My name is Rich. I'm a good guy. I swear we aren't mad about what you did to Eddie."

"Speak for yourself, Rich," a guy slumped against the wall groaned. The gunshot wound in his gut let me know this was Eddie. He whined and cradled his midsection with bloody hands.

Eddie must have been first down the stairs. It looked like Jared caught him in the stomach with the pistol. The small round would make Eddie's death slow and painful. That was good.

I moved off the stairs and slipped behind a stack of boxes. With all the yelling, these idiots had no idea I had snuck in behind them.

The men all had on similar masks, just like the dead one outside. Rich held a shotgun and the other a hunting rifle. Eddie must have been armed with some kind of weapon, but I didn't see it and he didn't look ready to use it.

"Go away or I'll shoot another one of you," Jared shouted through the heavy bunker door. I worried that he would make threats about me coming back soon and alert the men to my existence, but Jared kept it simple. Smart kid.

"Look, little man," Rich said. He tapped on the bunker door with barrel of his shotgun. "You have two choices. One you open the door and we all get real chummy. Or two, we light this house on fire and you cook in that box. Your call, my friend."

"Chummy?" the other man said. He let out a humorless laugh. "I'd like to get chummy with that chick he's got in there."

"Shut up, Jeff," Rich said. "You keep saying dumb shit like that and the kid will never open the door."

"Just speaking the truth," Jeff said. "You said we were going to enjoy ourselves."

"I know what I said, you idiot," Rich said. He shoved Jeff.

The men were missing patches of hair on the sides of their heads. Exposed strips of raw scalp glistened beneath the basement lights. Jeff turned and hacked a wet cough. He lifted his mask and spat a bloody wad of phlegm onto the concrete floor. These guys were dying and knew it. They just didn't know how soon.

There was no point warning these men or asking them to leave. I wasn't going to waste time with threats or negotiations. I stepped out from behind the boxes.

The roar of my shotgun in the small confines of my basement was deafening. Acrid clouds of spent gunpowder filled the room with a silvery haze. Rich lay on the floor with half of his face missing.

Jeff turned to fire, but fumbled with his gun. I racked a second shell and pulled the trigger. The lower half of Jeff's left leg turned to hamburger meat and splattered across the floor. He howled in agony and collapsed into the wet pile that used to be his limb.

I kicked Jeff's gun across the room and spun to face Eddie, who was still slumped against the wall. He raised his bloody hands.

"I'm not gonna fight," Eddie said. Blood ran down his hands and disappeared in the sleeves of his jacket. "I surrender." He tossed a small handgun across the room. I patted him down and found no more weapons.

"Stay still," I warned Eddie. I punctuated my sentence with the barrel of my shotgun. Eddie nodded his agreement.

Walking over to the bunker, I banged on the door with my fist. "Jared, are you in there? Is everything okay?"

"Lucas?" Jared asked. "Is that you?"

"Yeah, it's me," I said. The locks began to release from inside the bunker. "Jared, hold up. Don't come out yet. I need to take care of a few things. How's your mom doing?" Shooting someone in the gut was probably all the violence Jared's mind could handle today. The last thing I wanted was for him to come out, see the carnage splashed across the basement and lose it. Defending your mom was one thing. Picking your way through a bloody mash of meat that used to be a person was another.

The shock of seeing what another person could do to a body with a homemade knife or club was a daily occurrence in prison. I had seen my share of people turned into red oatmeal in prison. Jared didn't need this image knocking around in his head. Things were difficult enough already.

"Okay," Jared said. "I'll wait until you tell me to come out. My mom is about the same. She's sweating a lot and puked a few more times. Did you find medicine for her?"

"Yeah, I got it," I said. "Just sit tight." I turned back towards Eddie. Jeff was in shock and soon enough would bleed out. Once he was dead, I'd put my knife through the back of his skull to make sure he didn't turn into a husk, but I wasn't in any rush to take away his suffering.

"What do you want?" Eddie asked. He looked scared. That was good.

"You and me are going to have a talk," I said.

"A talk?" Eddie looked towards the hunting knife in my hand. "Then what's that for?"

I smiled.

A puddle of piss trickled out from beneath Eddie.

-24-

The color drained from Eddie's face. He wasn't going to last much longer. Jeff stopped moving and I no longer saw the spastic rise and fall of his chest. I buried the blade of the hunting knife in his temple, yanked it free and turned back to Eddie.

"What are you doing in my house?" I asked. Eddie groaned and pushed himself up on the wall. I knelt down to look into his eyes. His head lowered in an attempt to avoid eye contact. I pushed the barrel of my shotgun into the soft flesh between his chin and neck. "I'm not asking twice, Eddie." I stood up and pointed the gun into his face.

"We were just looking for supplies before we headed out," Eddie said. His words were breathy and forced. I figured I needed to make this quick.

"Supplies? How'd you know I had anything down here?" I asked.

"We didn't. I swear we had no idea." Eddie winced as I pushed the toe of my boot into his gunshot wound. "We were randomly checking houses before we left town. Then Rich saw the kid through a window and said we needed to check your house out."

Jared must have been watching for me. I couldn't really blame him. He must have been terrified of the possibility of his mother dying or worse, becoming a husk.

Seeing Jared is what drew Rich into the house. I suspected that these guys were after Danni, but there was no way they could have known she was in the basement. Connecting the dots, I saw that Rich's motivations had nothing to do with supplies. These men were filth. I needed Eddie alive, at least for a few more questions, but I couldn't fight the urge to kick him in the gut. Half my boot disappeared into his stomach. Eddie coughed a bright red spray of blood. Jared's shot must have punctured a few organs.

"So you saw the kid and came in looking for supplies, huh?" I growled. The shotgun trembled in my hands. While I was in prison, I tried to keep out of trouble, but once in awhile I would catch wind of a new inmate's crimes and I couldn't stop myself. Prison had its own justice system and pedophiles weren't tolerated.

"I don't get down like that," Eddie said. He was pleading. "That was Rich's thing. I was just with them because there was no one else. I just wanted to get out of town. I swear I wasn't going to touch the kid, not like that, I swear."

My eyes narrowed and the barrel of my shotgun rose to the center of Eddie's face without so much as a thought.

"Where were you going?" I asked through gnashed teeth.

"Out west, towards all those square states," Eddie said. He stopped to cough more blood. "Some guy has been broadcasting about there being survivors or something out that way. We were going to check it out."

I shook my head. They never would have made it. Their masks were shit and they were clearly a bunch of idiots and twisted fucks. That combination wouldn't have tilted the odds of survival in their favor.

The fact that they knew about Senator Heathway was problematic. I wasn't surprised that the senator had been broadcasting to anyone who would listen, but that meant that Danni and Jared wouldn't be alone on the road. I hadn't planned on   that.

"One more question," I said. "Was this your whole group? Are there more of you?"

"There were more," Eddie said. "We broke off into smaller scavenging parties. Some of us were in a few other towns. There was about thirty or forty of us, I think. We all worked at the auto plant. We snagged the masks from the paint department."

That was more people than Danni and Jared could avoid, especially if they were somewhere nearby and heading in the same direction.

I plunged the blade of the knife into Eddie's eye. There were at least three less that Danni and Jared would have to worry about on the road.

I wrapped the bodies in black trash bags and dragged them out of the basement. For lack of a better idea, I stacked them on the curb like I would on any other garbage day. The keys were still in the ignition of the Hummer. I pulled it around to the rear of my house and parked it next to the Bronco II.

Back in the basement, I did my best to clean up the pools of clotted gore. I used a hose and shop broom to sweep the red slop into the dry well. It would start to smell soon, but I could dump lye down there later and we wouldn't be staying much longer anyway.

I knocked on the door to the bunker. Jared stepped out.

"Is it safe?" he asked. He looked around the basement. Even though I had cleaned up, the violence was still apparent. Large black stains stretched across the concrete and the smell of gunpowder still hung heavy in the air.

"Yeah, we're good," I said.

"Did you get medicine for my mom?" Jared asked.

I handed him the 130 mg potassium iodide tablets. "Put one of these tablets in four capfuls of water. After it's soft, crush it. Then mix it into a bottle of water. After you're done with that, let me know."

"What are you going to do?" Jared asked.

"I left the bodies out in front of the house," I said. "It's probably not a good idea, especially if there's more of those assholes around. I'm going to drag them behind one of the neighbor's houses." I started walking towards the stairs and stopped. "Nice shot, by the way."

"I was aiming for his head," Jared admitted. "I shot him in the stomach by accident."

"It doesn't matter. You probably saved you and your mom's lives with that shot," I said. Even behind the NBC mask, I could tell Jared was smiling.

"Thanks, Lucas," Jared said. "For everything."

"No worries," I said. "Hey, by the way, how do you feel about a Hummer for your vehicle?"

"Those stupid boxy looking things?" Jared asked. "Aren't those for soccer moms named Tiffany or something?"

I laughed. "Yeah and you just got one. Congratulations, Tiffany."

-25-

The water in the bottle looked cloudy, but I didn't see any large chunks of the potassium iodide tablet. Jared had mixed it carefully. I swirled the water one more time to ensure that it was mixed.

"Help your mom sit up," I said. Jared helped Danni sit up on the bunk. She was slick with sweat. Her brown hair was matted to her head and stringy, but it looked like it was all there. I glanced over to her pillow.

"None fell out," Jared said, noticing where I looked. I nodded.

I held the bottle to Danni's cracked lips. "Come on, Danni, you need to drink this. Nice and slow. Just take a sip."

Danni forced a small mouthful of the water down and coughed.

"Tastes awful," she said with a dry laugh. Danni forced a second mouthful of the water down.

"Keep drinking," I said. "Finish the bottle and then get some rest." Danni nodded. I was glad to see that she was showing some signs of recovery. She must not have breathed in much of the ash, but it was still enough to make her sick.

"How was it out there?" Jared asked.

"Pretty much what you'd expect," I answered. "A lot of ash and even more husks. But the good news is that the roads looked pretty clear, so I don't think you'll have a problem getting out of town."

"Mom, Lucas got us a car," Jared said. He suddenly seemed so young and innocent. "It's a Hummer, but still, he got us a car."

"Yeah, you're welcome," I said with a snort. "But look, there's something else I need to talk to you about."

"What?" Jared asked.

"We can go over the specifics of it later," I said, "but those guys that were here are part of a larger group."

"Larger group?" Danni asked. Her voice cracked like it was out of practice.

"I talked to one before he, uh…well, before he died," I said. "He said that there were others in their group and that they were heading west."

"Isn't that where we're going?" Jared asked.

"Well, you are," I said. I didn't see a point in being dishonest. I had no intention of going with them to South Dakota. "But I'll make sure you've got all the supplies and guns you're going to need. You'll be okay."

"Can't you come with us?" Jared asked. He was doing his best to be strong for his mother and to prove himself to me, but I could see his fear.

"I can't, Jared," I said. I had to look at my boots. "I'm sorry, kid."

"I know," Jared said. He turned back to help his mother continue drinking the water and potassium iodide mixture. "I get it. You've got to find your wife and daughter, so you can't come with us." Jared's words weren't harsh or pointed. He was simply stating a fact.

"Jared," Danni said. Her voice was returning to normal, but she still looked sick. "Lucas needs to do what he feels is best. We'll be okay." Jared gave a quick nod and tilted the bottle.

"We'll lay low for a couple days," I said. "Danni, you need to rest and drink one of those mixes every day. I know they taste like crap, but it'll get you back on your feet." No one wanted to say it, but we were all relieved to see that although Danni might still be sick, she showed no signs of becoming a husk. "Let's eat a little something and then I want to reinforce the front door."

Later that night, I lay in my bunk. Danni and Jared were asleep. I felt my phone vibrate in my pocket. I rolled to my side and fished the phone from my pocket. The small screen cast a blue glow across my face.

Kara: Mom doesn't feel good. We're going out for medicine. Love you, Daddy.

My heart tightened and broke. Jagged shards lacerated my insides. I wanted to be there with Lisa and Kara. I wanted to be there to take care of them. I should be there. That was what a father and a husband was supposed to do.

I glanced at the keypad. It was black. I wished I hadn't broken the keys. I wished I had done a lot of things different. Most of all, I wished that I was with Lisa and Kara.

-26-

Lucas, how could you do that? Why would you waste our money on such stupid, pointless crap? What about Kara?

Lisa's words ran through my head on a constant loop. I dreamt the same dream most nights. It was our last conversation before she left me. I had screwed up the week's shopping by purchasing supplies for the bunker instead of the refrigerator. Lisa looked like she wanted to kill me. Sometimes I wish she had.

There's no way to argue with someone who can fire off questions like rounds from a machinegun. By the time I was answering the first question, four more were already on top of it. I sat in my kitchen and stared at Lisa. I knew I had screwed up and felt bad about it. I offered to fix it, to return something and get what she really wanted.

It's like living in a fucking fairytale, Lucas! I send you out to do something simple and you come back with beans! But these aren't even magic. No, you saunter in with a twenty-pound sack of dried kidney beans and have no idea why I'm pissed?

It wasn't true. I did know why she was pissed. I wished I could have made her understand why I was doing what I did. I guess sometimes even I didn't know why I did things. But I was doing them for her and Kara. Someday, we would need those beans. At least I thought we would.

Now I have to go back out in the rain to get milk and eggs and everything else that you left off your doomsday-shopping list. So help me, Lucas, there had better still be money in the account.

I thought there was, but I wasn't sure. I said nothing. Work had been slow and the time between paychecks was growing larger. I watched Lisa pull Kara's raincoat on and then the two of them walked out the front door.

Bye, Daddy! See you soon! Love you!

I told Kara that I loved her too. I loved them both.

Lisa and Kara never came home with the groceries.
I hated this dream.

-27-

The next morning Jared and Danni were still asleep when I woke up. The stress of Danni being sick stacked on top of being attacked had worn the two of them out. I slipped into my NBC suit, grabbed my mask and snuck out of the bunker.

The front door looked solid enough. I had reinforced it with some two by fours. It didn't look like anyone was getting in without letting us know. With the Hummer parked behind the house and the bodies moved to my neighbor's yard, I figured we were pretty safe. Whoever those guys were, one thing was clear – they were barely clinging to survival. They weren't an organized group. It was just a bunch of people that had worked in the same place and been lucky enough to grab some respirators. Even with the masks, they were dying. I hoped that they would all be dead before Danni and Jared head towards South Dakota.

The stairs leading up to the second floor of my house creaked with each step. I had told Lisa I would fix the stairs more times than I could remember. The truth was that I liked the sound of creaking stairs. It let me know that Lisa and Kara were in the house. It was the sound of a house that was filled with life.

Now, the sound felt closer to the whine of coffin hinges. There was still life in my house, but it wasn't the same. Danni and Jared were good people and I cared about them as much as I could, but they weren't Lisa or Kara. It was just different. There was no other way I could rationalize it.

More pictures of Kara and Lisa hung in the hallway outside of the upstairs bedrooms. I tried to avoid looking at them, but couldn't stop myself.

Dust coated the glass and gave the pictures a dull, hazy look. I used my glove to wipe away some of the grime. Kara's beaming smile broke through the grit like some long-forgotten treasure.

The next picture was from my wedding. Lisa and I didn't have the money for an expensive ceremony or party, but we had been happy. Younger versions of ourselves stood on the steps of the church smiling and surrounded by friends and family. We had been so full of hope and promise. Our lives had become intertwined and we couldn't have been happier. I don't know when we lost that feeling. It was something that slipped away bit by bit with each argument. It withered a little more each day we spent giving the other one the silent treatment. Looking back, I see how childish we had been. We were given the amazing gift of each other and then Kara, and we never stopped to think about how lucky we were. People could be so stupid. I had been stupid.

Life just got in the way. That was the truth of it, but it didn't make it any easier to accept. We wasted time worrying about bills and money. We stressed about saving more in the bank, even though we never would have enough to feel safe. So much time had been spent worrying and fighting about things that no longer mattered. The banks and bill collectors were gone. All that was left was our house and the memories it contained. That's probably all that ever should have mattered to us all along.

The door leading into Kara's bedroom was closed. The door was covered with pictures and artwork, all that had once been vibrantly colored, but that had now faded and curled. I gently touched a few of the sketches and paintings Kara had hung there. She had a real talent for art. Lisa and I couldn't draw anything beyond stick figures. But Kara had been an amazing artist from early on.

Memories of Kara's first week of kindergarten flashed through my mind. She had come home on Friday with a stack of artwork. An amazingly accurate painting of a cow caught my attention and I asked how much her teacher, Ms. Felder, helped her. I just couldn't see how such a little kid could paint it alone. Kara lost her temper and began screaming at me. I was shocked by her outburst, but she was enraged that I didn't think she painted it all by herself. From that day on, I knew better than to question my daughter's artistic abilities. I hung that cow painting on the fridge for months. Kara eventually made me take it down to make room for more artwork. She said it was babyish and demanded that I throw it away.

I pushed the door open to Kara's room. Dust coated the plastic that covered her things. After Lisa and Kara left, I kept the room immaculate. That was Kara's room, but it was my shrine to her. This was the museum of my daughter and I would visit it everyday after I came home from work. It was testament to the fact that I had been part of something amazing, that I had mattered.

I turned and walked across the hall to my bedroom. I lifted the plastic covering my dresser and pulled open the top drawer. Bunches of socks sat inside like an old clutch of dinosaur eggs. I pushed them aside and dug towards the bottom of the drawer. A wrinkled, yellow piece of paper lay buried beneath my socks. I grabbed the paper and walked back to Kara's room.

Sitting on Kara's bed, clutching a faded cow painting in my hands, I cried.

-28-

At some point, I must have fallen asleep on Kara's bed. An NBC suit and mask weren't exactly comfortable, but I was exhausted. My run to the pharmacy followed by a shoot out drained me.

The muffled shuffle of footsteps across carpet shook me from my sleep. Visions of a horde of husks surrounding the bed filled my head. I bolted upright and thrust the barrel of my shotgun into the nearest face.

Behind her mask, Danni's eyes were as wide as dinner plates. Her hands trembled at her sides.

"You shouldn't be out of bed," I said.

"Um, could you please lower the gun?" Danni asked.

"Oh. Yeah," I said, not realizing that I still had the weapon raised. "Sorry about that." I leaned the shotgun against the wall.

"I shouldn't have startled you," Danni said. She sat down next me on the bed. "I'm feeling better, not one hundred percent yet, but still better. Jared told me what you did to get me medicine and to keep him safe. Thank you, Lucas."

Danni did look like she was feeling better. She must have cleaned up in the decontamination shower that was set up in the basement. Granted, I couldn't see much of her behind a facemask and under a NBC suit, but she did look better.

"Don't worry about it," I said and shifted away from Danni a little bit. She sat down next to me, our legs brushing against each other's. The bed was small, but not that small. I moved a little further towards the end.

"Lucas," Danni said. I waited for her to say more, but she simply let my name hang in the air. I didn't know if she was waiting for me to say something or do something. I choose to stare intently at my boots as they left impressions in the carpet.

Danni's hand touched my shoulder. She gently pulled me towards her. I resisted and tried to inch further down the bed.

"Danni, what are you doing?" I asked, staring at the floor. She was beautiful. She was broken too, but still beautiful. Somehow that combination made her even more attractive. I pulled away. Complicating things further wasn't going to help anything.

"What's wrong, Lucas?" Danni asked. Her voice was husky and full of mischief. Her other hand settled on my knee.

"Whoa, whoa, whoa," I stammered and leapt up from the bed. "Danni, hold on. Look, we shouldn't…I mean we can't…"

"Why?" Danni asked. "Jared is downstairs asleep."

"No, not that," I said.

"Well, what is it then?" Danni stood up and moved towards me. She wrapped her arms around my waist and pulled me closer. "Is it the masks? I know we have to keep them on. It'll be kind of kinky." Her laugh sounded strange through her mask.

"No, it's not the masks," I said and gently pushed her away. *Was she really trying to seduce me while wearing a biohazard mask?* I thought. *Were people really into that sort of thing? Apocalyptic foreplay? If they weren't, I'm sure anyone left would be soon enough.*

"Is it your wife?" Danni asked. She sounded hurt, slighted maybe, but not angry. "I thought you said she left you. I thought this would be okay?"

"She did leave me, but I still love her," I said. "I'm sorry, Danni."

"I get it," Danni sighed. Her shoulders sagged and tears welled in her eyes. "It was a stupid idea. I just wanted to feel something…something, I don't know – normal, I guess. I just didn't want to feel like the world was over, even for a little bit."

"She did leave," I repeated, "but that doesn't change anything."

Danni was crying. I felt bad. I didn't know if it was the stress, my rejection or all of the above. I stood nailed to a spot on the floor.

"I wish I had met someone like you before all of this," Danni said. I studied her face. Was she still trying to seduce me? "Your wife was lucky to have you. I screwed up Jared's life so many times by hooking up with the wrong guy. I always seemed to meet the wrong one."

"Yeah, well there's a hell of a lot more of them. Stats just weren't on your side," I said. "Come on, let's go get some breakfast." Danni nodded.

It was easy to write Danni off as a weak female, desperate to latch onto a man, but that wasn't what was going on here. Danni was scared. I was too. She wanted to feel a respite from the ash-choked insanity that threatened to consume us both. Oddly enough, a recently paroled criminal with a doomsday bunker in his basement was the most normal person in Danni's life and all she was trying to do was feel something other than scared. I couldn't blame her for that. If not for Lisa and Kara, I would have been doing the same thing.

As I reached over to grab my shotgun, I saw Kara's cow painting on the floor. It must have slipped from my hands while I was sleeping.

Danni saw that I was staring at the painting, knelt down and picked it up. "You should hold on to this – hold onto them."

"Thanks," I said and tucked the painting into my pocket.

-29-

"So when do we leave?" Jared asked. He sat on the edge of his bunk, what should have been Kara's bunk, with an industrial-sized can of peaches cradled between his knees. I watched him swinging his feet in time with his chewing and realized how young he still was. Jared was just a kid and Danni was terrified. Could I really send them out on the road alone? I didn't want to be responsible for the bad things that might happen to them, but could I really forsake my own plans to ensure that they arrived safely in South Dakota.

No, I couldn't do it. I needed to see Kara and Lisa again. I didn't care that they left me. I was going to be with my family again and that was all there was to it. I would make sure that Jared and Danni were prepared, but that was where my responsibility ended.

"Your mom needs a few more days to recover," I said as I fished a peach-half out of the can and popped it into my mouth.

"I'm feeling better," Danni said. "You don't have to worry about us, Lucas. I know that you have your own family to worry about. You've done more than enough for Jared and me. Whenever you need to go, just let us know."

"You're still not coming with us?" Jared asked.

"I can't," I said.

"You mean you won't," Jared said. His face was pouty and only added to making him look his actual age.

"No, Jared," Danni cut in. "Lucas can't. He has to find his family. We have no right to try and stop him from doing that. You would do the same thing."

"I guess so." Jared stared into the amber depths of the canned fruit.

I opened my mouth to say something, what I wasn't really sure, but I felt like I should say something to Jared. The rumble of an engine sounded outside. I could hear the muffled roar in the street. It was something big. It sounded like a diesel engine.

"Stay here," I said and grabbed my mask and shotgun.

Creeping up the stairs, I edged around the side of the kitchen and towards the front of the house. I started towards the windows in the front of the house, but stopped myself. I didn't know who was out there and the last thing I wanted was to let them know that we were in here.

Skipping steps, I made my way upstairs and into my old bedroom. I knelt down by one of the windows and peered around the curtain.

A large flatbed truck idled in the middle of the street. Husks stumbled around the sides of houses and limped into the streets. People began firing on the husks with an array of weapons. The shots were sloppy, hitting the husks in the chest and limbs, but they fired enough to eventually clear the streets. I counted fifteen people, all armed.

I wanted to believe that this was some sort of rescue effort. It wasn't. Every one of the people outside my house covered their faces with the same masks that Rich and his men wore. They were looking for the missing part of their group.

Groups of twos and threes split off and began walking towards the houses on the other side of the street. They were searching the yards and homes. Soon, they would turn their attention on my house and find the Hummer in the backyard and then the bodies next door. I had seen enough.

I slipped out of my bedroom and made my way back to the basement. Jared and Danni could tell from the look on my face that the news wasn't good.

"What is it?" Danni asked.

"It's more of those guys, isn't?" Jared added.

"Yes," I said. "I counted fifteen of them. They're all armed and it looks like they are searching for the men I killed. It won't be long before they find the Hummer behind the house."

"What are we going to do?" Danni asked.

"We're going to stay down here until they leave," I said.

"But what if they find out that we're down here?" Jared protested. "The other guys did and I heard them threaten to burn the house down. These guys will do the same thing."

I grunted. Jared was right. These guys were going to find the bodies and the Hummer and it wouldn't be long before they found the bunker.

"Alright," I said. "I'm going out there."

"Then we're coming with you," Danni said. She moved towards the gun rack. Jared still had his pistol. I saw there was no arguing.

"Okay," I said, "but we have to have a plan."

-30-

Danni picked up one of my .45 caliber Glock pistols. She held it like a venomous snake that might strike at any moment.

"You're going to need to get over those feelings real quick," I said, pointing towards the handgun. I took the gun, chambered a round and checked the safety. "There's already one in the chamber, so when you're ready to shoot just make sure the safety is off, point and squeeze the trigger." I gave her a crash course in how to reload the gun and chamber a round. Danni nodded, but I could still tell she was scared.

"Don't pull the trigger, Mom, just squeeze it," Jared added. I was glad to see that he remembered some of the pointers I had given him. It still made me sick to think about bringing him into a shoot out, but what other choice was there? We needed to fight to stay alive. Life had always been that way, especially in prison, but it was never as crystal clear as it was now. These people were going to kill us if we didn't kill them first.

I picked up the second Glock and tucked it into a side pocket. My Mossberg was fully loaded and my pockets stuffed with extra shells.

A few other guns hung on the rack, but I didn't want any anyone to be loaded down. There were a few knives as well. Danni and Jared wouldn't need those. The last thing I wanted was to see Danni or Jared in a hand-to-hand combat situation. I grabbed a push knife and buckled its sheath around my belt. The knife was shaped like a capital letter T and had a double-sided blade. Holding the handle in my fist, the blade would extend between my middle and ring fingers. The blade wasn't good for slashing, but thrust into the side or back of someone's head, it was deadly. I figured it would work equally as good on humans or husks.

Images of Wolverine cut through my mind. Kara loved the X-Men movies and characters, especially Wolverine. I loved watching those movies with her, Lisa not so much, but she would humor the two of us. It was just nice to have everyone together. After the movies, Kara would run around the house pretending to be a mutant hero battling monsters and evildoers, slashing them with her imaginary claws. She never could have imagined how real that scenario would be some day.

"What's the plan?" Jared asked.

"Plan?" I muttered as I chased memories of Kara and Lisa out of my head.

"Yeah, the plan?" Jared motioned with his hand like he was talking to a toddler.

"Sorry," I said. "There are more of them than us, so surprise is our only advantage. I'll go out back near the Hummer. That way the side of the house and the fence will limit how many can get through at once. I want the two of you on the roof."

"I don't think I'll be able to hit much from up there," Danni said.

"Don't worry about shooting until you have to," I said. "I've got something in mind so you won't need to worry about aiming; just make sure you avoid our cars."

The three of us quickly went over the remaining details of the plan and headed for the bunker door.

Static popped and crackled on the radio at the far end of the dial. My first reaction was to ignore it and write it off as nothing more than white noise. Then Senator Heathway's voice came through and our entire plan went to shit.

-31-

"Lucas, Lucas, are you there?" Senator Heathway's voice rattled through the radio. *"I have amazing news, Lucas!"*

"What is it?" I asked. "We're kind of in the middle of a clusterfuck over here."

"Oh, I'm terribly sorry," Senator Heathway said, still very much a politician. *"I'll be quick then. We have made contact with a group of survivors in your area. They were taking refuge in an auto assembly plant on the outskirts of a nearby town. I let them know that there were other survivors in the area."*

"Did you tell them where you were?" I demanded.

"Of course," Senator Heathway said. *"Why wouldn't we? I gave them the coordinates yesterday. These people have a skill set that could prove quite useful, plus a large group means more security for everyone. I thought you might want to try and join up with them before they head our way."*

"You moron," I groaned.

"Come again, Lucas. I didn't hear that last bit," Senator Heathway said.

"You said it was a large group," I said. "Heathway, how many people are in this group?"

"I believe they said at least seventy," Senator Heathway answered. *"Lucas, why do you sound so agitated? I thought this would be good news."*

"Good news?" I said. Senator Heathway was desperate to gather survivors and rebuild some small piece of the world he understood. What he couldn't comprehend was that just because people were alive and had a certain skill set, it didn't mean they were good people. He was too busy dreaming of a new America and forgot about all of the problems of the old one, problems that had only been made worse by the husks and ash. "Heathway, listen to me. You do not want these people finding your group. A few of these people broke into my house and attacked my friends. I was forced to kill them and now more of them are searching my neighborhood."

"Lucas, I'm sure this is all a huge misunderstanding," Senator Heathway said. *"Just let me contact them and I'm sure we can iron these wrinkles out. Everything will be fine."*

"Is planning to assault a child and woman a huge misunderstanding?" I asked. The plastic of the receiver popped as my hand squeezed it. "You will not let them know about me. You got that, Heathway? Don't tell them anything. It's the only way we're going to survive this."

"You said that they were going to assault a child and a woman?" Senator Heathway sounded unsettled. He was beginning to comprehend the glaring mistake he made by rushing to trust these people. *"No, Lucas, that most certainly is not a misunderstanding. You have my word that I won't contact these people again. I'll alert the soldiers we have on patrol and tell them to be on the look out for a large group. Good luck, Lucas. Be safe."*

"Yeah, thanks," I said.

I hoped that Senator Heathway's word was good. We'd find out as soon as we went outside.

-32-

We snuck out the back door of my house. It opened off a small sun porch that was attached to my kitchen. When I built the sun porch, Lisa and I talked about Sunday morning breakfasts and summer nights with glasses of wine. Every plan we made was crafted with the best intentions. Like most people, we wanted to be happy and dreamt of ways to ensure that we would. Somehow life always seemed to get in the way and reality always won out. Things like happiness and love just didn't seem to fit into reality very often. We used the sun porch to store Kara's old bike and a million other things that never got used. After a while, we stored our dreams out there too.

The ash stopped falling from the sky about a day ago. Most of what was in the air had blown off the roof of nearby houses. A few husks stumbled through the powdery mess that covered my neighbor's backyards. A six-foot wooden fence ran around the edges of my yard. The husks stood ankle-deep in the ash, swaying and groaning dully. When they saw us standing on the steps, they became more animated and began to beat skeletal hands against the wooden slats of the fence. I wasn't worried about a few husks tipping the fence. It would take a lot more than what was back there. Danni was a different story.

"Don't look at them," I said as I tugged on the sleeve of her NBC suit. Danni was frozen. The attack had rattled her and made her even more scared. Seeing the leathery grins of the husks might be too much for her.

"Mom, I'm going out there and so are you. Lucas needs us to help him," Jared started down the stairs. Danni blinked as if awakening from a dream.

"Wait," she said. "Jared, wait for us." He stopped on the last step. Danni and I walked down to meet him.

"Come on," I walked towards the garage.

"I thought you wanted us on the roof?" Jared asked.

"I do, but not yet," I answered.

Inside the garage, we edged around the sides of the Bronco II and made our way to the back. I grabbed four wine bottles from the recycling bins in the back. Putting the blue buckets out had been something I forgot to do before going to prison. Now, I was glad that I hadn't.

"Hold these," I passed the bottles to Jared and Danni. Using the hand crank, I filled each bottle two thirds of the way with gas. Shredding a rag on my bench, I stuffed the frayed fabric into open mouths of the bottles. I took the bottles, put my thumb over the top and tilted them back and forth until the rags were soaked with gas.

I grabbed an old coffee can full of mismatched screws and nails and dumped it out on my tool bench. Normally, a mess like that would have bothered me, but I didn't have time to be anal-retentive. Attaching a few long strips of duct tape together, I pressed the sticky side into the screws and nails. Once it looked like a decent amount had been picked up, I repeated the process three more times and then wrapped the gray tape around the bottles.

"You want us to drop these from the roof?" Danni asked.

"Yes, but you're going to need to be careful. Wait for them to get into the back," I said. I looked at Jared. "How's your throwing arm?"

"I guess it's pretty good," Jared said. "I never was a baseball pitcher or anything like that, but I can throw a bottle."

"Hold it by the neck, light it and aim for their truck," I said. "But wait for them to come around the side of the house so they don't see you move to the front."

"What about me?" Danni asked.

"Aim for something hard so the bottle breaks and try not to set the house on fire," I said.

Back outside, I steadied the ladder while Jared and Danni climbed onto the roof. They could stay hidden on the backside. I moved the ladder back and kicked the ash around so there would be no clear sign of them up there.

Behind the Hummer, I watched the gate leading into my backyard. It creaked open and five men crept into my yard.

I took a deep breath and stepped out from behind the Hummer.

-33-

The first blast from my shotgun blew out the stomach of the lead guy. Blood and meat sprayed sideways like a morbid rose coming into bloom. The two men standing next to him were splattered with gore and stood dumbstruck. I wasn't waiting to discuss anything. I had seen how these people did things.

I fired off two more shots as the remaining members of the group turned to run. One screamed and fell to the ground. The springs on my gate pulled it closed. It bumped against the man's feet. It wouldn't be long before most of this group closed in on my yard.

On both sides of the yard, the husks were getting restless. The noise and smell of blood called out to them. Sections of fence shook as they battered their desiccated frames against it.

A heavy diesel engine rumbled in front of my house. The three men that escaped from my yard must have flagged down their friends.

The steely gray of the sky flashed the color of polished amber as a cloud of fire bloomed. Screams, erratic gunfire and black smoke filled the street. Jared had a pretty good throwing arm after all.

I couldn't stay cornered in my yard and figured the confusion out front would give me the best chance of moving undetected. The fence on the right side of my yard shook. The left side swayed a little, but not nearly as much. I jumped over the left side.

Three husks lunged as I thudded to the ground. One was missing its eye. The leathery skin looked scratched and puckered around a cavernous eye socket. A second husk dove forward. Its arms hung limply at its sides. The husk belly flopped to the ground. I kicked the third husk in the right knee and collapsed it beside its comrade.

The one-eyed husk stumbled forward, its teeth chattering and one remaining milky eye fixed on me. I pulled my T-shaped knife and drove it into the empty socket. With a twist and a second push, I felt the husk go limp. It slid off my blade and fell to the ground in an ashy cloud.

The husk with broken arms flopped on the ground like a recently landed fish. I stomped on the back of its neck and felt a satisfying *pop*. It wouldn't be dead, but it wouldn't be causing me any more problems either.

I turned my attention to the third husk. From the knee down, its leg hung uselessly. The husk tried to step forward, but having no recognition of its injury, collapsed to the ground. Pushing the husk's face into the grass, I drove the blade of my push knife into the soft spot between its neck and head. The husk thrashed and then went still.

A few more shots popped from the front of my house, but I didn't hear any aimed in my direction. A loud *whoosh* followed by a roiling black pillar of smoke bloomed on the right side of my house. They had to know that Danni and Jared were on the roof. I needed to move and draw the attention away from them.

Coming around the far side of my neighbor's house, I got a clear view of the street. The twisted remains of a large truck smoldered in the street. Human remains, as twisted and black as those of the truck, were scattered around the wreckage. Jared had great aim.

Behind the remains of the truck a handful of people crouched and fired wild shots at the roof of my house. Jared and Danni were safe on the other side, but without the ladder, they had no way to escape. Three men crept around the edge of the ruined vehicle. They were going to try and flank Danni and Jared.

Crouching low, I moved to the side of my neighbor's porch. A few sheets of lattice weren't going to stop bullets, but it kept me out of sight while I edged around to the steps.

From the porch, I could see more of the street. Shell casings glittered in tufts of ash like long-forgotten nuggets of gold. My roof looked pretty terrible, not that it really mattered. After this fight was over, there was no way we could stay.

Senator Heathway said there were seventy or more people in this group. Counting the dead, I wasn't even looking at half of their numbers. Three guys missing had brought this much attention. More than five times that many gone was definitely going to draw an even bigger crowd.

The three men edged around the truck and sprinted towards the side of my neighbor's house. It looked like they were planning on going over the fence and into my yard. What they weren't planning on was me hiding on the porch, standing up as they walked beneath me and firing off three rapid bursts from my shotgun. Ragged bits of meat that had once belonged to humans splattered across the ground. The ash, once gray and light, now looked like fresh tar as blood soaked through it.

The remaining men behind the truck turned their attention towards me and peppered the house with bullets. Bits of wood and splinters of plastic from cheap furniture rained down around me. I held my shotgun tight and rolled for the far side of the porch. I blindly fired back.

Under the metallic clamor of bullet casings falling to the ground, I heard glass shatter. At first, I took it to be one of the front windows being shot out, but that had happened almost immediately. Smoke drifted through the street. No more shots echoed between the empty houses.

Carefully, I looked over the railing. Debris from the porch clung to my NBC suit like snowflakes, but I wasn't bleeding. I slipped off the porch and moved towards the truck. Jared must have lobbed the last Molotov when he heard my shotgun fire. That kid could have played in the majors with that arm. Of course, he had a shit home life and the stands would now be filled with reanimated, leathery corpses instead of screaming fans, so that was kind of out of the question.

No one moved. The bodies smoked and a few still burned. I checked all the complete corpses, just to be sure. Screws and nails chewed through chunks of meat or become lodged in boney joints. It was unpleasant to look at, but I was glad the bombs had worked.

"It's clear," I shouted up to the roof of my house. "Danni. Jared. It's clear."

A muffled footstep thudded behind me. The gunshot cracked before I even had a chance to turn.

34

The gun slipped from Jared's hands and slid down the front side of my roof. It hit the gutter and spun out into space before falling to my front yard in a powdery cloud of ash. Jared's eyes were huge. Even from where I stood on the ground, I could see his eyes bulging behind the protective lens of his NBC mask. Tears welled and his shoulders hitched and heaved. Danni crawled up next to where Jared lay on the crest of the roof. She placed a protective arm around her son and drew him into a hug.

A body lay sprawled on the ground behind me. A small bullet wound on the side of the dead man's head wept blood, slowly turning the collar of his blue flannel shirt to an inky black. Three more wounds peppered his back; black puddles stretching sickly tendrils towards the one on his collar. A revolver was still clutched in the dead hands, the index finger still slipped around the trigger. I had never seen the guy coming up behind me. It was a stupid mistake, something I never would have done in prison. I had gotten careless. Jared hadn't. He was the only reason I was still alive to curse myself for being careless.

Around the back of my house, I steadied the ladder as Jared and Danni climbed down from the roof. Jared had stopped crying, but his eyes were still raw and red. Danni still had tears streaming down her face. I wanted to say something comforting, offer some sort of explanation, but what was there really to say? She had just watched her young son shoot someone. Sure, it had been to save my life, but I doubted that would make it any easier to stomach.

"Thanks, kid." It wasn't much and I knew it wouldn't offer any real comfort. "You saved my ass."

"I dropped the gun," Jared said. "Sorry, Lucas." He slowly worked his way down the ladder. Danni was close behind.

"Here." I held the gun out to Jared. Danni's hand moved towards it, but stopped and hung midair. She didn't want her son to be part of a world where he needed to carry a gun and kill, but like it or not, he was.

"Go ahead, Jared," Danni said. "It's okay."

Jared took the pistol and slipped it into his pocket. "I guess we're even now, huh?" he said, trying to make light of what had just happened.

"Yeah, I guess so, kid," I said. "You had to do it, you know that, right?" I didn't want this to eat at Jared, but knew that it would. I had killed people. Hell, that had been why I was in prison in the first place, but it was different for me. I was an adult. I had sufficient time to learn to rationalize shitty situations. Jared was still a kid. His mind hadn't hardened and become calloused like my own.

"Honey, he would've killed Lucas if you hadn't stopped him," Danni said. She was convincing herself as much as Jared.

"I know," Jared responded. He took a deep breath and squared his shoulders. He looked like he might be okay. I hoped that he would.

The fence on the other side of my yard shook. I watched a wave pass over the undulating wooden slats. Fingers wrapped in dried, yellowed skin grasped the top of the fence. The heads of at least twenty husks bobbed on the other side of the fence. Their dull moans drifted over the fence.

The smell of blood and sound of gunfire had drawn more husks into the surrounding yards. A worried looked passed between the three of us.

Wood protested and groaned as the fence posts splintered and broke. A large section of fence tipped into my yard. Husks swarmed over broken section of fence like cadaverous termites. More husks spilled through the opening.

Danni looked at me. Jared fired on the writhing pile of desiccated zombies.

"Run!" I shouted and pushed the two of them towards the house.

35

Thin fingers with skin like over-cooked, wrinkled hotdogs squirmed through the small gap between the door and its frame. I pushed against the door, trying to break the fingers and close it, but for every gratifying *snap* there were two more sets of digits. The husks had been drawn by the sound of dying men, the metallic tang of spilled blood and the promise of a meal.

Dull thuds echoed from the front of the house. Miraculously, the windows on the first floor had not been shot out, but a thin pane of glass wasn't going to hold up long against the relentless knocking of the husks. More shadows shuffled across my front porch and darkened the windows. It wouldn't be long before the husks were inside.

The rear door pulsed and pushed inward. I could hear the rear porch boards creak under the weight of the husks that swarmed my house. Jared and Danni ran to help me push the door back. Jared smashed at the leathery fingers with the handle of his gun.

"Danni," I shouted over the husks' charnel chorus, "grab a kitchen knife. Over there, in that drawer by the stove."

Danni rushed to the drawer and the door slid a little more open. Jared opened his mouth to say something, but slammed it shut and braced his shoulder against the door. Danni withdrew a long serrated knife from the drawer. I had used that knife to carve countless Thanksgiving turkeys. Kara and Lisa loved that holiday. There were less of the commercial expectations and more focus on spending time together. They were never huge football fans, but would humor me and watch the games. Holidays never evoked strong feelings for me, but I loved Thanksgiving because they did.

Slashing at the husks' fingers, Danni tore away ragged, dry strips of skin. I watched a yellowed knuckle bone flex as it worked into the open space.

"Get a bigger knife," Jared shouted. He smashed the handle of his gun against the boney joint. The finger popped and cracked before twisting to a sickening angle. The remaining digits continued to grasp for us as the now useless finger dangled and bounced before snapping free and falling to the floor by Jared's boot. I half expected the finger to inch across the floor like some sort of hellish caterpillar. It remained motionless on the kitchen floor.

Danni rushed back the drawer, grabbed a meat cleaver and ran back to the door. She hacked downward, removing fingers and chunks of palm. The husks showed no reaction and attempted to force the stumps of meat that had once been hands through the door. Danni swatted away the ruined limbs and pushed them back through the door.

Glass shattered in the front of the house. Something *thumped* to the floor of my living room. A second window broke. The shadowy outlines of husks squirmed over the broken glass like maggots covering road kill.

"Get downstairs," I spat through gnashed teeth as I forced the back door closed and bolted it. Lisa had always complained that the door needed a window, that the kitchen was too dark. I had promised her I would install a door with windows one day. I was glad I never did. The door shook, but held.

I stepped in front of Danni and Jared as they made their way to the basement door. Four husks shambled down the hallway. I aimed high, fired and watched their heads paint my walls with sickening sprays of white, red and black. More husks crawled through the windows to take their place. I fired another round into the living room and ran for the basement.

The basement door was cheap and hollow. It wouldn't last long.

"Come on," Jared waved from inside the bunker. There was nowhere else to go. I slammed the bunker door shut.

"We're safe." Danni collapsed onto her cot and pulled her mask off.

"We're trapped," I said. The words came out as if they were falling apart in my mouth. It was true that the husks couldn't get into the bunker, but we couldn't get out either. Eventually, we would run out of food and water. Our safe haven had become a tomb.

-36-

Silence filled the bunker like floodwaters. I could feel it slowly rising, weighing us down and threatening to drown the three of us. The steel doors muffled the sounds outside of the bunker, but we all knew the husks had taken over the basement and house. Moments before the bunker door closed, we heard the cheap hollow door at the top of the basement stairs splinter and break. The husks hadn't been far behind.

"Can't we just wait them out?" Jared asked. "I mean, won't they get distracted by something else and wander off? We've got enough food to wait until that happens."

"Maybe," I said. I wanted to assure Jared that he was right, but didn't see the point in fostering false hope. The husks in the basement wouldn't be able to navigate the stairs and probably wouldn't hear any sounds outside of the house. I envisioned countless, leathery death heads glaring at the door of the bunker, waiting for the slightest sign of a meal. The second they got that sign, the husks would surge forward and we would be dead.

"Well then what do we do?" Jared snapped. "Are we just going to sit here until we starve?"

"I don't know," I said. It was an honest answer and probably the last one that Jared or Danni wanted to hear. "I'm sorry. I'm out of ideas." I slid onto my cot and stared at the ceiling of the bunker. It was concrete, oppressive and gray. I hadn't come as far as I had believed. All I did was trade one prison cell for another. I was no closer to Kara and Lisa.

Danni and Jared shuffled around the bunk looking at the supplies and objects scattered throughout. There were no answers to be found, at least not the ones that they wanted. The gun rack loomed in the rear of the bunker. Danni pulled Jared away from the weapons.

We would run out of food and water, but we only needed three bullets. The thought was present in all of our minds, no one could deny it and our silence only confirmed it.

Danni and Jared climbed into their cots and tried to sleep. The scrape of countless leathery feet across the basement floor filled the silence that festered between us. We listened to the husks fill the basement. No one could sleep, but we had nowhere to go. We were trapped.

-37-

At some point during the night, I must have fallen asleep. I woke to an oppressive blackness and felt a flutter of panic pass through my heart and head. Jared or Danni must have turned the lights off. That was all. Nothing else had happened. I listened to them snore softly.

My right pocket vibrated.

Kara: Hi, Daddy! Mom is feeling better. See you soon? Love you!!! ☺

I squeezed the phone. Why did my keys have to be broken? Where was the justice in that? Plastic popped. I relaxed my grip and stared at the screen. I couldn't stand those stupid little smiley faces and pictures that Kara and Lisa always found some way to work into a text message. They tried to get me to use the things. I resisted until I found the smiling swirl of poop. After that, Kara and Lisa were okay with me not using them.

The urge to smash my phone ripped through my mind. I hated that I was stuck, locked away from my wife and daughter again. But smashing the one thing that kept me connected to them would only punish me. I took a deep breath and let the phone slip from my hand.

Across the bunker, the radio crackled and popped.

"Lucas? Lucas? Are you there? Is everything okay?" Senator Heathway's voice rattled through the radio. I thought about ignoring it. I wanted to blame him for our current situation. I wanted to blame anyone other than myself.

"Lucas, are you going to answer Senator Heathway?" Danni asked. Her voice was rough and heavy with sleep. Jared stirred on his cot. I wish I had turned the radio off.

"Screw Heathway," I grunted. "I'm going to sit here until the husks rot and fall apart and then I'm getting the hell out of here."

"But who knows how long that could take," Danni protested. "Shouldn't we at least see what Senator Heathway wants?"

I let my feet hang over the edge of my cot before dropping to the floor. There was no point in talking to Senator Heathway. Whatever he wanted was sure to involve us not being trapped in a bunker in my basement.

"Lucas, are you there? There have been some developments with the monsters. Lucas, are you there?" Senator Heathway asked again. Through the radio, his voice sounded like a hysterical robot. *"Lucas, please answer me. I promise you that I had nothing to do with those men who attacked you. I need your help. We all need your help. Please."*

I dropped into the chair in front of the radio. A heavy sigh slipped between my lips as I picked up the receiver.

"I'm here, Heathway. What do you want?" I grumbled.

After hearing his response, I wished that I had stayed asleep and never answered.

-38-

"He said that the rest of those people were heading for them, right?" Danni asked after I tossed the radio receiver aside. Senator Heathway had given that group coordinates and the rest of them were heading towards them. He was an idiot.

"Yeah, he did," I groaned. I rubbed the bridge of my nose, suddenly exhausted and my eyes burning. "And he's a moron. What the hell does he expect us to do about it? He's got half an army there, I'm sure he'll be fine."

"But Senator Heathway said that most of the soldiers left. He said there was some kind of disagreement or something. It's mostly woman and children there now. They won't be able to fight off that many people. We can stop them," Jared said. The kid was an optimist, I had to give him that. "We stopped them two times before. I'm sure we could do it again."

"Kid, there are three to four times as many people in the main group," I said. "They are probably all armed and I'm sure won't be too happy about us trying to stop them. Besides, how the hell would we even get out of here to stop them? I'm sorry, Jared, but this is Heathway's problem. He made this mess and he'll have to clean it up."

"But if they get there and take over, it'll be gone," Jared argued.

"What will be gone?" I asked.

"Our chance," Danni cut in. "Lucas, if they take over or destroy Heathway's settlement, we'll have nowhere else to go. We'll be stuck."

"We are stuck," I snapped. "We're stuck in here with a shit ton of husks on the other side of the door – all waiting to make us dinner. And you heard what Heathway said – the husks aren't rotting. The radioactivity or something has preserved them like beef jerky. I thought we could wait them out, but we can't. All we can wait for now is to run out of food. I'm sorry, but it's over. Heathway is screwed and so are we."

"What about your wife and daughter?" Jared asked. His question blindsided me like a sucker punch. I shook my head, but Jared's question refused to stop echoing in my mind.

"What about them?" I asked with more intensity than I intended. Jared stumbled back a few steps and held his hands up.

"I was just saying," Jared continued, "that if we're stuck in here, how are you going to see them again? That's what you wanted, right? Ever since you got out of jail, all you've been talking about is seeing them again. And now you're suddenly going to give up on that? How are you going to do that locked in here?"

"Jared, stop it," Danni admonished him. "Don't talk about Lucas' family. It's not our business."

"I'm not saying it to be a jerk," Jared protested. "It's the truth, though."

"Jared, that's enough," Danni's voice seemed shrill and pointed as it echoed in the small bunker. "Lucas, I'm sorry. Jared doesn't know what he's saying. You've done nothing but help us ever since this started."

"It's okay," I muttered. "He's right."

I leaned forward and rested my head on the table, hoping that a change of angle might loosen some idea in my mind. I pictured my thoughts moving through my head like one of those blue wave machines that shrinks always seemed to have on their desks.

Something rattled loose and bounced through my mind like a pinball. It was a bad idea, probably one of the worst ones I had ever had, but it was also the only one I could think of. I would do whatever it took to see Lisa and Kara again, even if I might die doing it.

-39-

I threw together three backpacks with supplies. I know some people had their Bug-Out Bags on standby, but I never really gave much thought to abandoning the bunker. It was probably poor planning on my part, but the truth was that I never planned on leaving the bunker because I never planned on leaving Kara and Lisa. I stocked it with everything we could ever need. The bunker was ready for every disaster and emergency – except of course an undead horde of radioactive monsters.

But Lisa and Kara weren't with me. Danni and Jared were and that was different. I felt responsible for them and cared about their safety, but it wasn't the same as what I felt towards my own family. How could it be? With Kara and Lisa outside of the bunker, there really was no reason for me to stay any longer. We could try and wait out the husks and probably had enough supplies that we could make it with a little rationing, but if what Senator Heathway had told us was right, there was no waiting them out.

A few CDC scientists had drifted into Senator Heathway's camp a little before the soldiers left. With little else to do, they spent their time studying husks and trying to figure out some sort of cure or vaccination. So far there wasn't one. What they had discovered was that the husks weren't rotting. They figured that bugs would take care of the rest, but after awhile even the insects burrowing through the husks' died out. The flesh was dead, but it wouldn't rot. The only explanation was that the radioactivity had somehow preserved them and rendered them basically bug-proof. There was no waiting the husks out.

"So we're just going to open the door and let the husks in?" Danni asked. I could see the worry and doubt plainly written on her face. Jared had been silent ever since I unveiled my plan. I think he was trying to prove his bravery. I hoped he wasn't going into shock.

"That's the plan unless you've got a better one." I handed Danni her backpack and then passed a second to Jared. "We needed to be ready to run in case my plan goes to shit." It was probably more appropriate to say *when* it went to shit because I really didn't see any other way something like this could go, but Danni and Jared were frightened enough already.

"Okay. We're not going to let them all in, right?" Danni asked. She took a deep breath and picked up her gun. Something was changing in Danni. I'm not sure if she was hardening or if she was just getting used to the insanity of our world, but she suddenly looked less afraid. I was going to ask, but saw her cast a quick glance at Jared. I had my answer. She was getting ready to protect her child. It was the most basic and primitive instinct a parent could feel. It was exactly what she would need to get through this.

"We're going to do this controlled," I said. "We let in one or two at a time and use our knives to kill them. Aim for the temple and push until the husk stops moving. Then we move the body to the back and do it again. We'll try and thin the numbers a bit before we venture out into the basement or use any ammo. No guns, unless you have no other choice. Thanks to Heathway, I get the feeling that we're going to need every bullet we've got."

The three of us shared a series of worried looks. There was probably something Danni or I needed to say to reassure Jared, some thin white lie about how we were going to get through this, but he had seen enough to know what we were facing.

"Here." Jared passed my NBC mask to me and then handed one to Danni. He slipped his over his face. "Let's get this over with."

There was nothing else to say.

-40-

The bunker door opened with a muffled *whoosh*. The sound always reminded me of opening a can of Pringles. Eating was one of the last things on my mind. Not being eaten on the other hand, well that was pretty much the only thing.

The dull moans rattling from the dried throats of the husks filled my basement. I did a quick count. It looked like there were about twenty husks. That was twenty more than I would have liked to see waiting for us, but it was still less than I had anticipated. Some of the husks must have crawled back upstairs, which would mean they'd be waiting for us. I pushed that thought out of my head as the nearest husk lunged for me. I grabbed its thin neck and yanked it into the bunker.

I had never seen any signs of emotion in the dull milky eyes of the husks and their leathery faces were permanently fixed with a revolting smile, but I could have sworn a moment of surprise flashed across that creature's face as I slammed it to the concrete floor and Jared plunged a blade into its skull. Danni grabbed the husk by its boney ankles and dragged it to the back of the bunker.

"One down, millions to go," I joked. No one laughed. I shrugged. Humor had evidently died as well.

I pressed my shoulder against the door and pushed as Jared grabbed the nearest husk and pulled it inside the bunker. The cracked yellowed teeth gnashed together as the monster tried to tear meat from Jared's arms. Danni stepped forward and plunged her knife into the side of the husk's skull. It went limp on the floor.

Fingers wrapped in cracked, yellowed skin clawed at the air between the heavy bunker door and the jamb. I pushed harder, but felt my boots slipping. I was losing ground to the countless husks that battered against the other side of the door.

"Little help," I growled and pushed harder. Danni rushed behind me and pushed.

"Jared, clear the way so the door can close," Danni said.

Jared took a step towards the door before stumbling and howling in pain. He lay on the floor, his gloved hands rubbing his ankle. The husk on the floor crawled towards him.

"Jared!" Danni cried and let go of the door.

"Help me get the damn door closed!" I yelled. Danni hesitated, caught between the danger outside of the bunker and the one inside that threatened her son.

"Mom, close the damn door!" Jared shouted. Danni turned and helped me push it closed. I felt the light crunch of finger bones caught between the door and frame as I spun the handle to seal the door.

By the time I had turned around, Jared had killed the husk. It lay motionless on the floor.

"Jared, are you okay?" Danni asked. Large, glassy tears glistened in her eyes. "I'm so sorry. I thought it was dead."

"It *was* dead," Jared snorted. "That's why they're zombies, Mom."

"Jared, this isn't the time for jokes or bravado," Danni said. Her voice was stern, but still trembled with bottled emotion. "You were bit."

"My suit was bit," Jared argued. "I'm fine. It hurt, surprised me, but it didn't break through. I'm fine."

Danni tried to say something, but her words came out choked and short. She grabbed Jared and hugged him.

A thin trail of blood ran down the side of Jared's boot. I saw it. Danni didn't. Maybe it was just a scratch. Maybe it was a bite.

"Come on," I said. "Let's keep going."

There really was no other choice.

-41-

The husks were thin and withered. Nothing more than leathery skin wrapped around bone and desiccated organs. The stack of bodies in the rear of the bunker reached the edge of the first bunk.

Danni grabbed the next husk Jared passed her. It slipped off the pile and bumped into the back her legs. A startled yip echoed inside Danni's mask. She spun to face the husk, her knife raised. It remained motionless.

"Just throw it on the bunk," I shouted. The seconds I spent turning to yell were enough for the husks to force the bunker door open a little more.

"But," Danni hesitated. "On the bed?"

"Mom," Jared snapped. "We're not staying here after this. No one is sleeping on that bed."

Danni grabbed the husk and heaved it onto the bunk.

"Little help," I growled and pushed the door. Jared rushed forward and threw his weight against the door. Small puddles of blood trailed behind him. The kid was hurt.

"Jared," I said. He saw where I was looking along the floor.

"Later," Jared snapped. He shoved the door.

An arm, like the branch of a diseased winter tree, slipped through the opening and grabbed for Jared. The skeletal fingers slipped through the straps on the side of Jared's mask and yanked towards the door.

Jared swatted and pulled at the fingers. I reached out to grab Jared's shoulder, but the bunker door pulsed inward. I was on the floor. The ceiling rippled and pulsed as my head bounced off the concrete floor.

Somewhere in the distance, I could hear Jared struggling and cursing. I could hear Danni screaming as she rushed past me. I pushed myself up from the floor and watched her disappear into the seething mass of undead monsters that swarmed over her son.

-42-

Before my mind went blank, I must have said the words 'get down' or at least some close approximation. I really hoped that I did.

The remaining husks were knotted together in the middle of my basement. Somewhere in that tangle of dried out dead flesh and teeth was Jared and Danni. As I pushed up from the floor of the bunker, words spilled from my mouth. They felt heavy and chewed. My tongue was thick. My head packed with cotton. I pawed for my shotgun, swatting at empty air and cold concrete. Something heavy and cold brushed the tips of my fingers. I snatched it from the floor and stood on shaky legs. My vision was watery, but at this range and with a shotgun, aiming didn't really matter. It didn't so long as Jared and Danni were down on the floor. If I didn't fire, it wouldn't matter either.

The concussive *BOOM* of my shotgun echoed off of the cinderblock walls. Normally it would make a person's ears ring, maybe even cause a temporary loss of hearing, but I barely noticed the sound. The only thing I wanted to hear was Danni or Jared. Not the dull moan of the husks or the dry scrape of their leathery feet across the floor. I needed to hear the two of them, to hear that they were okay.

I felt something vibrate in my pocket. My cell phone jumped. Kara and Lisa were trying to contact me. The keys were broken and I never would be able to respond. I still wanted to read the message, even if it would cause me pain, even if it was bad news. The grip of my left hand loosened on the pump of my shotgun. It wanted to drift to my pocket, to grab my phone and flip it open.

I shook my head and forced my fingers to tighten and rack another shell. I fired again and then again. Clouds of gun smoke drifted through the basement. Wide, wild sprays of black clotted gore painted the gray walls. My gun was empty.

The last husk pawed for Jared. Danni lay across her son, shielding him from the monster. I stumbled forward, raised my gun and smashed the stock into the back of the husk's head. It lurched forward and splayed across the concrete floor.

The husk scuttled towards Jared like some mummified spider from the tangled corners of Hell. Danni's knife plunged into the back of the husk's skull. The force of the blow drove the zombie against the floor.

Danni's eyes were wide and shot with red veins. Small clouds of blood crept from the corners of her eyes. I couldn't tell if she had been screaming or crying. It was probably both. Jared shifted beneath her. She instinctively pushed him back down and tried to cover him.

"It's over," I muttered. "Danni, it's over."

She looked around the basement. Slowly, she stood up.

Jared climbed to his feet. They were both covered in blood and bits of gore.

"I'm okay," Jared said. It sounded more like a question than a statement. A deep gouge ran down the side of Jared's head where the husk had pulled at his NBC mask. Blood ran from the wound and clotted in his hair. It looked painful, but not serious.

Danni shook, her knees buckled and she collapsed to the floor, surrounded by husks. She used her boots to push the desiccated corpses further away from her. Each body left a thick snail's trail of spoiled blood as it slid across the floor.

"Mom, are you alright?" Jared asked. He knelt next his mother. "Mom? Were you bit?" She had used her body to shield her child. I wonder what that move would cost her.

"Does it matter?" Danni asked. Her words were thin. "Bit? Not bit? It doesn't make a difference. It doesn't matter."

"What do you mean?" Jared demanded. "Of course it matters."

"No," Danni answered, "it doesn't matter. We're going to die anyway. I see that now. How can I protect you in this world when I never protected you before?"

"Mom, stop." Jared stood and tried to pull his mother up with him. "It does matter. Of course it matters. Right, Lucas?"

"I...uh..." I turned to walk back into the bunker. "I need to check my phone. Kara needs me."

"Lucas?" Jared asked weakly. "Lucas!" I could hear the anger rising in his voice. I couldn't bring myself to care.

"Sorry, kid. My phone." Covered in chunks of spoiled flesh and fragmented bone, I climbed onto my bunk and opened my phone.

-43-

I walked out onto the front porch. This used to be where I'd sneak off to smoke a cigarette after I promised Lisa that I'd quit. Once Kara was born, I actually found the reason to quit. Kara became my reason to do a lot of things.

Fatherhood was strange like that. I spent the majority of my life thinking that I knew what I was doing and why I was doing it. I was an adult as far as I could tell. Then Kara arrived and I realized that I didn't know my ass from my elbow when it came to life.

There had been nine months to prepare, but I figured that was more for Lisa than me. I figured that I wasn't going to have to change, not really. I don't think I had ever been more wrong in my life.

Sitting on the porch at night always helped to clear my thoughts, to clear out all the crap from the day. Tonight, I was finding it harder to dump the day's bullshit. Lisa left for the supermarket and took Kara with her. I was supposed to go earlier in the day. A sack of rice and dried beans weren't going to cut it. Lisa had been pretty pissed – she had been pissed at me plenty of other times, but this time I didn't seem capable of shaking the feeling.

A light rain began to fall. October was almost over and the rain was cold – even under the protective overhang of my porch I could feel the chill of invisible fingers plucking at my bones. Still, this was one of my favorite times of year.

Halloween was one of the few holidays my family agreed upon. Granted, Lisa always wanted Kara to be something cute, some new Disney princess or a pumpkin or some other taffeta shrouded nightmare. But this year was going to be different. This year Kara had finally been old enough to choose her own costume. Lisa tried to sway Kara, to get her to agree to be the latest cartoon fairytale heroine. Evidently, my genetics were stronger when it came to

Halloween costumes selection. Kara wanted to be a zombie, but not just some cheesy, green-faced monster in thrift store rags. She wanted to look like a REAL zombie. The kid had done her research. Lisa protested, insisting on the princess. Kara flat-out refused. Realizing she was never going to win, Lisa sought middle ground and suggested that Kara dress up as an undead Disney princess. I don't know if my smile or Kara's was bigger. The three of us worked every night after dinner for damn near a week. It was going to be great.

Screaming echoed from next door. My neighbor, some lady and her kid, had moved in a while ago. Since then I had seen a merry-go-round of men go through those doors. None of them lasted more than a couple of weeks. She seemed okay, I guess. Maybe a little needy, but otherwise okay. The kid seemed pretty together, though Lisa had said he looked lost.

I listened to something smash. It sounded like a plate, maybe a lamp. I wondered who had thrown it. There was more yelling. Now I could hear the kid's voice too. Something else broke. It sounded like he was defending his mother.

I took a few steps down the porch stairs. There wasn't much thought in the action. Hearing that kid defending his mother stirred something in the back of my mind, some part of me that had woken up with the birth of Kara. I knew it was going to be a lopsided fight and the kid could use my help.

Halfway across the lawn, my cell phone started vibrating in my pocket. I snatched the phone and looked at the ten digits blinking on the screen. The fact that it was a number let me know that I probably didn't know the person and sure as hell didn't want to talk to them. Disappointment stabbed at my heart. I guess I had been hoping that it was Lisa calling to let me know that she had forgiven me and was coming home. I sent the call to my inbox and slipped the phone back into my pocket.

A dull thud echoed from one of the front rooms in my neighbor's house. More screaming. A lot of crying. I couldn't hear the kid anymore. Anger surged in my gut and made my head swim. I didn't know who was in that house. I didn't care.

My phone leapt and twitched in my pocket again. Angrily, I wrenched it from my pocket. The same ten digits blinked on the screen. No telemarketer or auto-call machine would dial me twice in such a short time, not unless they wanted the Better Business Bureau shutting them down.

"Who is this?" *I demanded.*

They answered and I wished that I had never asked. Somewhere in the distance I could hear shouting, things breaking, more crying, but my brain had shut down. I couldn't think. I couldn't move.

I blinked and life skipped a few frames. There was no more screaming. I wasn't outside. I was sitting behind the wheel of my car speeding towards a destination that I would have given anything to avoid.

Two patrol cars shot past me. Some Good Samaritan on my street must have called them. The cops were headed for my neighbor's house. They weren't coming for me.

Not yet.

-44-

"Lucas, we're leaving," Danni said. She shuffled around the bunker throwing supplies into her backpack. Jared was busy doing the same. He hadn't uttered a word since I climbed onto my bunk.

Kara: Daddy, I don't think me and Mommy can wait much longer. Are you gonna be here soon? I miss you. I think Mommy does too!

I stared at the phone. Its dark keys mocked me, a dark lighthouse as I was lost at sea.

"Lucas, I said that we're leaving," Danni repeated. "You need to come with us." She had obviously recovered from the shock of getting attacked by a horde of husks.

"I need to?" I asked without looking at her or Jared. "I don't need to do anything other than see Lisa and Kara again. That's all I need to fucking do. You want to leave? Go ahead, but I'm not going anywhere."

"What about those people?" Jared asked, breaking his silence.

"What about them?" I snapped. "Just stay off the major roads. It looks like they're traveling in large trucks and there's a lot of them. It should be easy enough to avoid them. There's a radio and maps in the Hummer. The preset channel is programmed to Senator Heathway's frequency. Radio him if you need help or get lost."

"Isn't there a radio in your truck?" Jared asked.

"What's your point, kid?" I asked.

"Shouldn't one of the preset channels be programmed for your radio too?" Jared glared at me. He asked a simple question, but his words were loaded and sharp.

"Channel 2 is." I stared at my phone. "Call Heathway if you get lost."

"Lucas, please come with us," Danni said.

"I already told you! I'm not going anywhere!" I rolled away from them. With my back turned, I didn't see Jared leap for my

123

bunk. Before I knew what he was doing, he had snatched my phone.

"It's blank?" Jared asked. He pushed the keys and buttons on the side. "It's dead. Lucas, this phone is dead."

I leveled my pistol with the center of Jared's head. I wasn't proud of it. In all honesty, I didn't even really think about it. I just wanted my phone back.

"Jared? Honey, let me give Lucas his phone back. It's probably just the battery." Danni slipped the phone from her son's hand. She passed it back to me, but not before she looked at the screen and dark keys. "Here, take it. We'll go."

"But it's blank, Mom," Jared protested. "How can Lucas talk to his daughter on a phone that's dead?"

"You must be mistaken, Jared. Now stop," Danni said. Her words were sharp and caught Jared by surprise. He opened his mouth, slammed it closed and shouldered his backpack.

I watched Danni and Jared walk up the basement stairs. The floorboards creaked as they made their way out of my house. I listened to the back door slam. The Hummer rumbled to life. My phone vibrated.

Kara: Daddy, did you get my last message? Are you coming to see me and

Mommy? You know where we are, Daddy. We're waiting at our spot. Hurry up,

Daddy.

It wasn't dead. The phone worked. Jared was pissed off and scared, that was all. The message was right there in front of me. The keys were broken, but the phone worked. Jared didn't know what he was saying. Fear had gotten the better of him.

"I'll be there soon, baby girl," I whispered.

I closed the phone and slipped it into my pocket. My own bag waited for me in the corner by the door of the bunker.

I threw the bag over my shoulder and took the stairs two at a time. Once I was out the back door, I cast a quick glance at my house. This house had meant so much, had protected the things I held precious. None of that mattered anymore. I was going to see my family.

Deep tire tracks cut across my yard leaving deep furrows in the ash. I could hear a few husks groaning behind a section of fence that hadn't yet collapsed. It would fall soon enough. None of this mattered either.

I threw my bag onto the passenger seat of the Bronco II. I was leaving.

-45-

There had been so much blood – more than I would have thought a human body could hold and still he was breathing. The human body truly was an amazing machine. It could be abused and destroyed, but would still keep working, could still heal and rebound from whatever had been done.

A wet cough gurgled in his throat. Red bubbles burbled and frothed around the edges of his mouth. He rolled to the side and vomited blood onto the pillow. The stark contrast of the blood on starched white pillowcase almost looked artistic, something that could be framed and hung in a New York museum. Pollock would have approved.

I wondered if he would be able to heal, not that I cared. This man, whoever he was, didn't matter anymore. What mattered was what this person had done. What could never be undone.

I barely knew this man's name, had only recently learned that this person even existed. How could I hate someone so completely when I had only recently learned of them? When only a few words had been uttered between us? It had been less than a day since this person entered my life. In those few hours, he had irreparably altered everything I thought to be true, everything that I held dear. Still, I hated this man with such clarity – such resolve that it should have scared me. It didn't.

Outside of the room, nurses and other hospital staff rushed past the room. A police officer was supposed to be stationed outside the room. He must have stepped out to use the bathroom. It would have been much harder to get in here if he had been where he was supposed to be.

The television was on, the sound leaking out of the tinny speaker attached to the bed controls. I couldn't hear it. Some housewife that was more plastic than human staggered around in a cheap glittery dress spilling wine on her children and laughing.

The kids look traumatized. How could anyone sign a kid up for that? Anyone who would didn't deserve to be a parent.

Maybe I didn't deserve to be a parent either.

Someone shouted outside of the hospital room. Muffled footfalls rushed down the hallway. I could hear someone yelling at me, commanding me to do something. Pain exploded in the back of my skull. A blinding burst of stars exploded from the corners of my eyes. It was dazzling, almost beautiful.

Handcuffs clicked around my wrists and pinched my skin. More people rushed past me as I was pulled from the room with my hands locked behind my back.

The stars flickered and faded under the sickly neon lights of the hallway. I watched them blink out of existence. I had watched too many things do the same earlier tonight.

Errant gusts of wind scattered ash across my windshield. I pulled the handle back to spray washer fluid, but it only created a thick paste for the wipers to smear and made the problem worse. I tried a few more times to clear my view and cursed as it continued to get worse.

The CB radio that hung from the underside of dash crackled and a garbled voice drifted through. I reached over to turn it off, but found myself unable to turn the dial all the way to the left. I never should have even turned the stupid thing on. Who was I going to talk to? Senator Heathway was a moron that had made his own fucking bed and I sure as hell was in no rush to make it mine. Danni and Jared knew what they were getting when they teamed up with me. My goal was never a secret. But then why had I turned the radio on in the first place?

"Damn it," I grumbled.

Danni and Jared were okay, I'm sure they were. I had given them supplies, directions, guns and a truck. That was more than anyone else had going for them. And they could easily avoid those assholes from the auto plant that were heading towards Senator Heathway and his people. Besides, from what I had seen, those guys weren't in good shape and probably would keel over before they got too far.

"Lucas?"

It was Danni.

I shook my head. I should have turned it off. I never should have turned it on.

"Lucas, are you there? Please, Lucas."

Why was Danni radioing me? They left hours ago and should have been getting close to being out of range. With all the crap in the air, they shouldn't have been able to radio me at all.

Reaching for the radio, I took my eyes off the road. The Bronco II bounced and pitched to the right as something smashed into the front bumper. I wrenched the steering wheel back in the other direction and fought to keep the truck on the road.

Through the greasy gray smear of ash that caked my windshield, I could see a husk clawing its way across the hood of my truck. The damn thing must have been wandering around on the edge of the street and leapt for my truck when it heard the noise. The husk was missing everything from the waist down, the impact having severed its legs. A thick, black ropey tangle of intestines dangled from the lower half of the husk like the tentacles of a jellyfish, leaving zigzagged trails in the ash. It beat skeletal hands against glass and repeatedly lunged for me with broken, brown teeth.

My NBC mask sat on the passenger's seat. As I reached for it, a second and third husk scrambled onto the hood of my truck. The mask slid to the floor and wedged itself under the seat. I was eye to milky eye with three reanimated leathery corpses.

Small cracks spread across my windshield like the weavings of invisible spiders. One husk never would have gotten through, but three focused on one spot were a problem.

I stopped my truck and put it in park. I tugged on my mask, but it snagged on something. The husks continued to beat on the glass. I couldn't risk going outside without my mask and firing through the glass was out of the question. A few seconds was all I needed. Just a few seconds to get my mask free.

An idea, a stupid, stupid idea bounced through my head. A dry laugh echoed strangely inside the cab of my truck as I turned on my windshield wipers. Thin lengths of rubber and plastic whipped back and forth on metal arms slapping the husks' hands and faces. I couldn't stop laughing and momentarily worried that I had finally snapped, but crazy people never worried about being crazy. Right?

One husk lunged for a wiper, missed and slid off the hood of my truck. The remaining two zombies clung to my truck. Glass creaked as they both pressed in on the same area.

My mask came free. I slipped it over my head and rolled down the driver's side window. The smear of ash across the glass provided cover. The husks continued to attack the glass and wipers, completely unaware of my shotgun. I hung out a little further and pulled the trigger.

Spoiled black gel splattered across the hood and windshield of my truck, glistening in the ash like fresh droplets of fresh tar. I let out a strange laugh as my wipers continued to smear the disgusting mix across the glass. My laugh was cut short.

The world tilted and I watched as my feet slid out from the driver's side window and pointed towards the sky. Pain exploded in my back as I crashed onto the pavement. Stars danced and hot pangs of stabbing pain radiated through my body.

The smell of blood and the sound of the car wreck would call to the husks. They would be here soon. I wasn't sure how much longer I would be. I tried to push myself up, to bring my feet beneath me so I could stand, could flee. My legs felt heavy and useless.

"Lucas, please pick up! We need your help!" Danni sounded panicked.

"Stop looking at your stupid phone!" Jared sounded angry. *"Lucas, it's broken. I don't know where your family is, but they aren't on the other end of that phone. No one is. I saw the screen. It's blank. Please, we're here and we need your help."*

My head rolled to the side. A hill rose at the end of the street, an island breaking through the ash and destruction that surrounded it.

The phone in my pocket vibrated, but I didn't need to answer it to know who was calling me. Lisa and Kara were waiting for me at the end of the street.

-47-

GUILTY. I don't remember hearing the word. I don't remember the expression on the judge's face. I did remember Lisa and Kara. They were all I could think about as I was handcuffed and escorted out of the courthouse. I was placed in a van, and two hours later, I was sitting on a wooden plank bench in the intake room of my new home.

The prison had a name, but does that really matter? No matter what name you gave the place it was still a prison. I think it had some former warden's name honorably tacked on before the words 'Correctional Facility.' I never understood that phrase. How was locking all of the worst people together with nothing to do beyond getting worse going to correct anything? Don't get me wrong, most of the people in here deserved to be locked up and had no business being loose in society. But if it was going to be called a Correctional Facility, one would think they would at least make an attempt to correct the things that had landed us there in the first place.

I didn't need to be corrected or fixed or whatever. I wasn't like the other inmates. My crime wasn't about money or respect or being crazy. What I did was justice.

My first night in prison I couldn't sleep. There were too many people around me, too much wasted life crammed into one place. Sleep and me had never really gotten along, not until I met Lisa. Then Kara was born and I never really slept again. I spent the entire night thinking about them. It was the worst feeling I had ever experienced.

I never wanted to be away from them ever again.

-48-

Something heavy pressed my wrist into the ground. My other arm was also trapped. I couldn't get my shotgun around and the husk was climbing closer to my face. Its broken, jagged teeth chattered as the monster tried to find purchase in soft flesh. I thrashed and tried to knock the husk off of me, but I was pinned to the ground. From the corner of my eye, I could see a pile of heavy debris – chunks of rock, a few car parts and other things with weight piled on top of my arms. Had I passed out? How had this happened?

Somewhere off to my left, I could hear laughing. It was soft and feminine, almost like Lisa's laugh. I loved her laugh, though our life together seemed to rob her of it. But this laugh was different. It held notes of joy, but they shared nothing with the memories that Lisa and I had fostered together. I wanted nothing to do with whatever wrought this kind of joy, though I doubted that I would have a choice.

"You're tough. I'll give you that." The laughing carried on for a few more seconds. Boots shuffled around me. The steps were heavy, clumsy, but different from the dragging march of the husks. These people were alive.

"Who's there?" I knew the question was pointless. What did a name really matter? It could be the Easter Bunny and still wouldn't change the fact that they had pinned me to the ground with half a husk on my chest.

Hands grabbed the husk. I craned my neck and could see two men in paint respirators holding the monster at bay. Their gloved hands clutching exposed rib bones like the handlebars of a bicycle. The breathing masks told me everything that I needed to know.

"You're the one that killed Eddie and the rest of our friends," the voice continued. "I heard what you did when we sent some people over to check things out. Honestly, I'm kind of impressed and glad we finally got a chance to meet."

A woman stepped into view behind the two men holding the husk in place. She had a solid build and square shoulders, her hair chopped into a messy nest of straw-colored spikes. Icy blue eyes glared from behind a pair of safety glasses. She held an automatic pistol in one hand, a meat cleaver clutched in the other.

"You're Lucas, right?" she said. The meat cleaver turned over in her hand, as if in consideration of my answer. "We heard about you over the radio. Call it luck, but we had plenty of supplies in the car plant, even an old HAM radio. Seems one of the late night janitors screwed around with it on his breaks."

"I'm guessing that moron Heathway told you that," I answered. "Remind me to thank him later."

"Actually," she continued, "you might just get the chance to do that depending on how you answer the next question."

"Which would be?" I shifted my feet and tried to angle my hips to buck the husk from on top of me. One of the men laughed and pushed my leg down with his knee.

"Well," she said. "Here's the thing, you killed a good number of our friends, which should really piss me off. And don't get me wrong, it does, but here's the thing. You seem to really know what you're doing, how to handle this clusterfuck of a world. So you agree to come along with us, help us make it out to Heathway's settlement and I'll let you thank him however you see fit."

"Lady, no offense," I answered, "but who the hell are you and why would I want to help you? The first thing I knew about your group was when three of your people broke into my house to do something terrible to my neighbor's kid. Not exactly the best introduction."

"Fair enough," she shrugged. "My name is Courtney Darby, but most people just call me Dar."

I tried not to laugh. This mountain of a woman, hands calloused and curled like two baked hams, was named Courtney. I could understand why most people called her Dar.

"Look, Lucas," Dar continued. "If you haven't noticed, things have changed. Those guys were looking to let off a little steam, destress. Who am I to judge how they do it?"

"You won't need to," I said. "I did."

"You're not one of those born again, preachy types are you?" Dar feigned concern. "I might need to retract my offer if it means that I'd have to listen to you preach the entire way to South Dakota."

"No," I answered. "I just do not have tolerance for sickos."

"The world is sick, Lucas," Dar said. "People are just the byproduct of it. Always have been. Always will be. Don't over complicate things." She spun the handle of the meat cleaver. "By the way, I'm glad you mentioned that kid. Seems the rest of my people found them on the interstate in my friend's Hummer."

I told Danni and Jared to stay off the major roads. The abandoned cars would have been bad enough. Knowing that this group was possibly on the roads and still using them was a death sentence. Why had they been so stupid? Why had I?

They were never going to make it to South Dakota alone. They must have been scared; trying to put some distance between them and whatever else they ran into. The interstate probably seemed like the best option.

"So what's it going to be, Lucas?" Dar was getting impatient. So was the husk.

"Get me up," I said.

"Glad you're a reasonable man," Dar nodded.

"Because I can't kill you from down here," I finished. "It'd be much appreciated if you could help me out with that."

"Kill me?" Dar laughed. "That's great."

"No," I said, "that's a promise."

"A promise?" Dar aimed her gun at my head. "Promises are for sleepovers and deathbeds. I guess the second isn't too far off. Last chance Lucas."

"Just shoot me already," I answered.

Dar shook her head. "Too bad." She turned to the two men holding the husk. "I'd love to watch this deader strip your face. These two will get that pleasure, but I've got to get moving. Heathway was trying to sell some bullshit about the settlement being overrun – that it wasn't safe anymore. I'm sure it's got nothing to do with you filling in a few blanks for him regarding us. Can't wait around for him to gather reinforcements." Dar let out another laugh. "Be seeing you, Lucas." She nodded to the men, "Let it go."

-49-

The husk scrambled across forward, its leathery fingers clawing the fabric of my NBC suit. One of the men wanted to take my mask, but Dar stopped him. Felt it would be better to allow the zombie to chew through the plastic, give me some more time to think about how stupid I had been.

The two men watched – their laughs muffled by the cheap respirators covering their faces.

"Ten minutes," one said.

"Ten? He won't last five," the other answered. They were taking bets on how long it'd take for the husk to kill me.

Boney points dug into my suit, a blunted pain blossoming with each grasp. I bent my knees and forced my feet flat on the ground. My shoulders screamed in protest.

"Look he's starting to squirm," one of the men laughed.

"Like a worm on a hook," the other added.

I pulsed upwards and twisted my hips to the left. The husk tumbled off and landed on the cracked asphalt with a dry *thud*. With no legs, it struggled to right itself. There would only be seconds to get free.

Pushing off the ground, I swung my legs over towards the pile of debris pinning my left arm. I pushed and wrenched my arm free. One of my captors rushed forward. I drove both of my feet into his lead knee. As the joint popped and twisted to an unnatural angle, he screeched and collapsed to the ground. I freed my other arm.

The second man lunged forward, a hammer raised in a half swing. I waited for him to get closer. Launching from a low crouch, I drove my shoulder into his gut. The hammer collided with the lower right side of my back, but most of the swing's force had been lost. He stumbled backwards, tripping over his fallen friend. The hammer spun across the cracked macadam.

"Please," he begged, holding his hands out defensively.

There was nothing to say. The decision had already been made. I picked up his hammer. "Consider yourself the lucky one." The clawed side of the hammer connected with the top of his head. A sickening bolt reverberated through the handle of the tool. I wrenched it free and let him fall to the ground. He sputtered, drool and blood mixing. Then he was silent.

Turning my attention to the other man, I pointed with the gore-caked hammer. "I'll give you three."

"Three?" he asked. "What are you talking about?"

"Minutes," I answered.

After a few minutes of heavy lifting and a few well-placed hammer swings, I had the second man pinned to the ground. The husk continued to scuttle forward, pulling itself along like a slug. I would let it get close before pushing it back with my boot. I wanted him to know what was waiting for him.

Confident that the man was securely in place, I picked up the husk and tossed it towards him.

There were a series of screams. Something wet popped and snapped. Then nothing. Three minutes was a bit of an overestimation.

-50-

My Bronco II was wrecked. Dar and the others took most of my supplies. I scavenged what I could. A few dented cans of food, a handgun, a small medkit and some other odds and ends, but nowhere near what I previously had in my truck.

Kara: Daddy, we're waiting for you.

The bag slipped from my shoulder and fell to the pavement. I turned the .45 over in my hands, as if it were the first time I had ever held a firearm.

Kara: Daddy?

The hill loomed at the end of the street. Kara and Lisa were waiting for me. I slid the gun into my bag and threw it over my shoulder. My steps stuttered a little as I walked past the cab of my Bronco II. The dome light was dark. The battery must have been cracked in the crash. I imagined Danni or Jared's panicked voices pleading through the tinny receiver, begging for help, for me.

I was glad that it was silent, unsure of whether or not I could have ignored their voices. My feet were heavy. Radio or not, I was still ignoring Danni and Jared. I knew they needed help.

This wasn't my problem. At least I tried to believe that it wasn't. I never asked them to join me in the bunker, never told them that I would be responsible for them. I told them I would help them get on the road and I did that. My job was done.

Since my parole, all I've been trying to do was get to Lisa and Kara and now they were a few blocks away. Jared and Danni would be okay. Everyone was responsible for themselves that's how this world worked. Hell, it worked that way before the husks showed up. It was simple human nature.

I forced my boots to move. I hadn't come this far to stop.

-51-

It rained most of the day. I watched through the small window in my cell. Somewhere dirt was being thrown. Somewhere sod was being rolled into place.

I couldn't be there. I was never going to be there again.

The man sleeping on the bunk above mine snored softly. The weather kept us inside and sleeping helped pass the time. I still hadn't adjusted to the new routine. I still wanted to be outside.

I longed to stare into the rectangular voids that received the remnants of my previous life. More than that, I longed to throw myself into them. To disappear. To be done with this life that was beyond repair – let my sins and worthlessness slowly rot away beneath six feet of dirt.

Many inmates dealt with similar feelings. Every so often the guards would find someone pale and dangling from the bars in his cell. I couldn't fault them, but I wouldn't be like them. I wouldn't let this place by the last thing that I saw. I would survive, serve my time and find my family.

I would see Kara and Lisa again.

The gates to the Brookview Cemetery hung slightly ajar. I was surprised to find the grounds empty. No husks stumbled between the markers or clawed free from the spongy earth.

A laugh fogged my mask. I had watched too many zombie movies. There was no reason for the husks to pay attention to Brookview. There was nothing to eat and as far as I could tell you had to be alive before whatever made you a husk did its dirty work. A cemetery was probably one of the safest places to be.

I walked the rows, unsure of where to look being that I hadn't been allowed to attend the actual funeral. I remembered buying the plots and vaguely remembered the numbers.

"Sixty-five A through F," I read from the small bronze signs that sectioned off the cemetery. A few more to go.

The row waited for me. My girls waited for me. I stumbled between the stones, desperate to find Kara and Lisa.

Two spots waited a little more than halfway down the row. They looked no different from the hundreds that surrounded them. Simple gray stone, slick with rainfall, jutted from the ground, a plant of pure despair grown from the cadaverous seed planted beneath them. A small depression in the ground pooled water over each grave.

Lisa never liked the idea of buying grave plots. I liked to be prepared and never wanted Kara to worry about making the arrangements. The thought of me not being in one of the plots never crossed my mind. But here I was standing in the rain, a day similar to the one when the graves were filled. Lisa and Kara were gone and I was here. It was by far the cruelest punishment I had suffered.

The ground was soupy. I sat there, letting the water pool around my legs, my mind drifting back to prison. Frank should have let that other inmate stab me. He would have been doing me a favor.

There was nothing left for me out here. I had fooled myself into thinking otherwise.

I slipped the NBC mask from my head. Rain cascaded down my face. A cold breeze drifted between the gravestones. It felt good to feel the air, to breathe something other than the musty air of my basement or my own stale breath. There was always the chance that whatever created the husks was still in the air, but I figured that I wouldn't be around to care if it still was there.

My phone vibrated.

Kara: Daddy? Are you coming to see Mommy and me?

"Soon, baby girl. Very soon." The pistol trembled in my hands. My teeth clicked against metal. I could taste oil and the tang of spent gunpowder.

Kara: Daddy?

-53-

The phone in my pocket vibrated, trembling in time with my frantic heartbeats.

Kara: Daddy, stop. Stop, Daddy. I love you.

The pistol splashed to the ground. A muddy pool began to form around the edges of the weapon as it sunk into the spongy earth.

"I love you too, baby girl." The screen of the phone was blank. The keys were dark. "I love you." Greasy drops of rain smeared across the cracked screen. There was no message. Nothing had come through since I was released from prison. Whether it was memories of old messages, insanity or a combination of the two, there had been no messages.

I had been looking for permission to end my life, but wasn't going to find it here, not from Kara or Lisa. They were gone and I was still here. It was cruel. It was real. If I was lucky I would see them again, maybe in some spiritual sense, but that was never going to happen in this graveyard and I wasn't going to unlock the Pearly Gates with a round from my .45.

Something hitched in my throat. I swallowed hard, but found no relief. Tears stung my eyes. A sound, unlike any I can remember making, echoed between the gravestones.

Water pooled around the gun, around me. It had been a long time since I had cried and I was unsure if I would be able to stop, be able uncurl my knees from my chest and stand again.

My phone vibrated.

"You're not real," I moaned, snot streaming down my face. "You're not real."

Kara: Daddy, stop it. Mommy and I love you, but Jared and Danni need you.

I don't know if I believed in Heaven, I still don't. But any chance was better than no chance. Hell seemed pretty real lately, so maybe there had to be a counterpoint to balance the equation.

There was a pretty long list of bad things in my book, I knew that much. It was probably time I started balancing that out.

I pulled myself to my feet, my hands trembling as I gripped Lisa's grave marker. I stopped to gently kiss the tops of the two stones jutting from the ground before me.

I was probably crazy, probably had been since I lost Lisa and Kara. Prison didn't help either, it never does. But I would rather be insane and still connected to the people I love, than sane and utterly alone.

Kara: Good, Daddy. Now go help them. ☺

That damn smiley face.

Help them. Kara and Lisa wanted me to help Danni and Jared. Like I had been unable to do for them. I couldn't save my girls. They were gone, but there was still time to save Danni and Jared.

My girls waited for me. They loved me and I would see them again. Until then, I need to give them a reason to keep waiting, to keep loving me.

My NBC mask sat between the two graves, a small piece of myself left with Lisa and Kara. It was probably stupid and sentimental to do so, but I had been taking in lungfuls of air since I arrived at Brookview. Whatever sickness or poison or whatever was in the air either was already in me or was no longer toxic. Either way, it didn't matter. I picked up the .45 and headed for the cemetery gates.

-54-

Husks swarmed over the remains of my Bronco II like maggots on road kill. There wasn't anything left in there anyway. I shouldered my bag. Something seized in my chest. My throat hitched. A long string of black mucus dangled from my chin as a cough doubled me over. I spat it to the ground.

The spit pooled in the divots left by a set of tires. My eyes followed the tracks. A few husks stumbled through the ashy streets, their feet burying the trail. A length of rebar jutted from a pile of random junk. I wrenched it free and connected with the nearest husk's head. The monster lurched sideways, falling to all fours. Its head was collapsed inward, bits of yellowed bone poking through the leathery skin, but it was far from dead for a second time.

Stepping over the downed husk, I continued down the street. These tire tracks were left by Dar's people. It was my best chance to find Danni and Jared.

On foot, I was making decent time, but the husks were starting to notice and I found myself leading a morbid parade of reanimated corpses down the center of the street.

A mountain bike lay on its side. The blue paint shone through the greasy coating of ash that clung to the frame. A desiccated body was tangled around the metal and gears. I put one foot on the rear tire and pulled the corpse free. It came free in two pieces, loose bits rattling to the sidewalk.

The pedals groaned and gears protested as I pushed down. A mechanical *chunk chunk* clanked as I steered the bike into the middle of the street and shifted gears. It was less than ideal and slower than my Bronco II had been, but it beat the hell out of walking and would keep a healthy distance between the husks and me.

I glanced over my shoulder to see the husks stumbling along. A few dropped away from the pack, easily distracted by other sounds or movement. The front tire of the bike traced the lines left by the tires. Dar's people had vehicles, but wouldn't be able to travel too fast as they scavenged supplies. They were ill equipped and would have to stop frequently.

I'd catch up to them. I'd find Jared and Danni – because I had to, because Kara and Lisa wanted me to.

-55-

A line of vehicles snaked their way through a snarl of wrecked cars on the highway. A heavy-duty pick-up truck led the way, its candy-apple red paint shining in stark contrast to its surroundings. Husks lunged from where they were trapped, the metal twisted into makeshift sarcophagi. A large moving truck, the type anyone could rent, but no one had any business driving, dominated the middle of the convoy. A black Hummer brought up the rear. The supplies strapped to the top marked it as Danni and Jared's vehicle. There were more people than I wanted to deal with, but it was still less than I expected.

I had scavenged a pair of binoculars from a burned-out sporting goods store. The case was slightly warped, but the lenses were still in good shape. I watched the convoy come to a stop. Five cars had crashed and turned sideways across the lanes of traffic. It would take a while to move these or they'd have to double back to the nearest exit ramp, either way this was my best chance.

Stashing the mountain bike under an overpass, I listened to the arguments taking place on the highway above me. It sounded like most wanted to try to push through instead of doubling back.

"Screw that," a voice shouted. "We're not getting off the highway. It's a wasteland down there. You saw what happened in the last town. Dar said that we stay on the highway, so that's what we're doing."

"Dar's not here, you moron," another argued.

Good news. Bad news.

I had the right group, but they had apparently split up. As much as I wanted to save Jared and Danni, I really wanted to take Dar out. They would never be safe as long as she was guiding her people towards Heathway and his settlement in Buffalo.

No matter. It was better to get things done in small steps. One thing at a time.

The screech of metal and a chorus of cursing let me know what their decision was. I hopped on the bike and peddled for the nearest on ramp. It wasn't far, but I'd have to move fast.

The ramp was choked with more wrecks. I ditched the bike and climbed over a dented-up sedan. A husk thrashed in the driver's seat, the seatbelt lashing it in place. A coating of black, hardened gore covered the seat beneath the husk from where skin and meat had sloughed away. It flaked and cracked as it struggled against the seatbelt. The stench inside of the car must have been overpowering, not that the husk appeared to mind, but I was glad that the glass was still intact.

I dropped off the hood of the car and ducked behind the nearest wreck. A few hundred yards up the highway, Dar's people worked on pushing through the wall of cars. The red pick-up had moved off to the side. It looked like the driver didn't want to damage the ridiculously oversized chrome brush guards and paint job.

A few people stood at the rear of the group. Most of the group appeared to be men, but there were some with smaller frames that could have been women. It was hard to tell with the respirator masks and missing hair. Patches of raw scalp glistened where clumps of hair had slid off. Stringy deadlocks dangled where the grease and dirt clung to the remaining strands of hair.

I grabbed a chunk of concrete the size of a tennis ball and tossed it at a group of cars a few yards away. It clanked off the roof and rolled underneath a nearby car. Three husks stumbled around the sides of the cars, clawing at the air, teeth gnashing.

"Over there," one of the people from the convoy pointed.

"Take care of them before they attract any more. No guns. We're making enough noise already."

I waited.

Two of Dar's people headed towards the husks. Edging around the surrounding cars, I crept closer. I still had the hammer from before. The metal had gone from a shiny nickel finish to a dull black.

The first of the two walked past me. As the second passed, I swung the hammer in a tight upward stroke. The soft space underneath his chin absorbed the blow, throwing his head backwards. A muffled grunt slipped from beneath the mask as he collapsed to the ground. He dropped a knife. It was a large cheap kind, sold in the kitchen sections of big box stores. I buried the knife in the neck of the second man and wrenched in backwards until the handle snapped. There was a spray of blood and wet gurgle. I rolled onto the trunk of the nearest car. The husks took care of the rest.

A riot-style shotgun and a hunting rifle jutted out from the writhing pile of feasting husks. I leaned over and used the claw end of the hammer to pull the guns towards me.

Once I had the weapons, I dropped off the side of the car and scrambled through the nearest open door. Images of the trapped husk raced through my head, but the car was blessedly empty. I shut the rear passenger door as a husk collided with the glass.

I checked the weapons. The shotgun had been sawed on both ends and looked like it was more electrical tape than gun. It would probably jam or explode in my hands. There were five shells.

I was luckier with the hunting rifle. It was a Browning BAR. Someone had envisioned themselves as a big game hunter or was at least the type of person who felt they needed a semi-auto hunting rifle capable of firing magnum rounds. A few heavier rounds were slid into the bandolier on the strap. Four regular rounds were in the gun.

I had never been much for hunting. Survivalist sure, but not really hunting, though I figured the line between the two had become increasingly blurry.

Slipping between wrecked vehicles, I carefully took my shots. The first few caught the rest of the group off guard and thinned their numbers, but surprise only lasts for so long when the sound of your rifle has the grace of a drunken dinosaur. Still, it was a good weapon and I was happy to have it.

Four were left – people, not rounds. I loaded a few of the heavier rounds into the rifle.

"Just leave," I shouted from behind a car.

A shot *pinged* off the hood in response.

"I'm not asking again," I added, not really sure that what I said mattered one bit. "I just want the girl and the kid back. Give me a vehicle and tell me where the rest of your group was headed and you walk."

A second shot chewed a crater into the street off to my left. These idiots were terrible shots, but they also didn't appear to be wasting ammo either, so I had to think fast. Sooner or later, they would get ballsy and try to flank me.

Flank me? That was it. The obvious choice for them was to split up and come at me from both sides. Shadows bobbed behind two sets of cars on opposites, as if in agreement with my summation. If flanking me was their plan, then going straight forward had to be mine.

I tucked the sawed-off shotgun into my NBC suit and scrambled under the car in front of me. I watched boots scuffling behind other cars, edging closer to where I had previously hid. I kept crawling forward.

Two men remained near the pick up and Hummer. They apparently weren't as dumb as I first thought. Each one watched a side, completely ignoring the middle – ignoring the danger that crawled towards them.

"Don't send those MENSA applications in just yet, fellas," I muttered as I lined up my shot.

A pink haze wafted about as bits of skull bounced along the pavement like hail. The first one dropped to the ground. By the time the second realized where I was, it was too late. I lined up a shot and blew out his left knee. He howled in agony and writhed next to his dead friend.

I rushed forward and kicked their guns away. It looked like two big box deer rifles – nothing special, but certainly better than nothing.

The gunshots alerted the remaining two that something was wrong. Cut off from their vehicles and no one watching their backs. Something was very wrong, indeed.

"We're leaving," one of them placed his gun on the hood of a car and backed away. "Just leave us…I mean please, just leave us the keys to whatever truck you don't want."

"Yeah," the second added, dropping his gun to the ground. "Just like you said before, you want to find the girl and the kid. Just keep heading west towards South Dakota. Dar's using the main roads. She'll be easy to track. You find her and I bet you'll find that lady and the kid."

"See," the other one added. "We're not so bad. We're doing like you asked."

"I said I wasn't asking again," I clarified and fired two quick shots.

"South Dakota," the last one gasped. Shock was setting in. He stared at his ruined knee, hands trembling, as if unsure of how to even begin to attempt to address the injury. "Look what you did."

"Let's not focus on the past," I said. "Just keep talking and you might be walking...oh, sorry. I guess hopping out of here."

"Just like the others?" he sneered.

"I told them I wasn't asking again," I answered. "I'm nothing, if not honest."

"You're a psychopath," he added and spat a wad of bloody phlegm at my feet.

"Yeah, maybe." I withdrew the sawed off shotgun from inside of my NBC. "So you should probably think very carefully and make sure that the next thing out of your mouth is what I want to hear."

"Dar took the woman and her kid," he said. "I'm not sure what she did with them or why she even wanted them, but that's where they are. She's taking them with her towards that politician's settlement in Buffalo. Stick to the main roads and you'll find them. Okay?"

"Fair enough," I shrugged. I studied his face for a few moments. It looked like he was telling the truth, but something was off. The majority of his face was hidden behind a respirator mask, but what skin was visible had a sickly hue. The lines of his face appeared hardened, maybe even cracked. Eyes, deep-set and bloodied, glared at me.

"What's wrong with you?" I toed him.

"You mean other than the fact that you blew my kneecap off?" he snapped.

"Yeah, asshole," I nodded. "Kneecap aside, what the hell is wrong with you?"

He coughed and tugged at his mask. "Nothing's wrong with me."

I snatched the mask from his face. The surrounding skin flaked and peeled, some still attached to the purple plastic of the respirator. A ring of leathery red skin traced the outline of where the mask had sat.

"Like Hell nothing's wrong with you." I looked at the tattered skin that fluttered around the edges of the mask. "Disgusting." I tossed it aside.

"Dar says we're fine as long as we keep our masks on most of the time," he said. His gums were black, lips cracked and bleeding.

"Dar's full of shit," I answered. "And whatever the hell is floating around out here has already done whatever it was going to do. Your piece of shit painter's mask didn't do jack, other than slow it down."

"So what's that mean?" he demanded. "Are you saying I'm going to become a rotter?"

"Rotter? Husk?" I shrugged and looked at a few of the monsters stumbling towards us. More would be here soon. "Maybe. I guess so? Or maybe you'll just die a slow, painful death. It's not like I really know what the hell is going on around here lately or really care what it does to you."

"Shoot me," he pleaded. "I don't want to be one of those things."

"One of those things?" I asked. "You're already something worse. It'd be a waste of a bullet."

Two vehicles waited, their engines idling. As much as I wanted to take the pick up and leave that ridiculous Hummer to rust on the side of the road, I didn't have time to transfer the supplies from one to the other.

"Looks like you're getting the pick-up truck," I said and pulled the keys from the ignition.

A tangled knot of husks stumbled between the wreckage, drawn closer by the smell of blood and fresh meat. Some stopped to tear chunks away from the cooling bodies, but they didn't appear to hold the same attraction that we did and more closed in.

"Give me the keys." He grasped at them in my hand.

"Keys?" I asked.

"Yes, the fucking keys!" he shouted. "Give them to me before the rotters get here. You said I get the pick-up. Give me the keys!"

"You do get it," I nodded. He appeared relieved, but before he could speak I added, "Yup, you get the truck. But I don't recall saying anything about the keys."

I tossed the ring of keys into the approaching mob of husks.

"You probably shouldn't trust a psychopath. Enjoy the truck."

-58-

The Hummer was boxy and made me feel like a soccer mom, but the oversized chrome bush guards helped push two cars far enough apart that I could turn around and back track to the ramp. Husks grabbed at the vehicle as I pushed my way back towards the ramp. I could have run them over, given that guy a chance at survival. Then again, he could have decided to leave Danni and Jared alone. He could have decided not to join Dar. I'm sure every person following her had some variation of the same hollow story, a slightly different flavor of bullshit to justify hurting someone else. I had seen it more times than I could remember in prison. And I could almost guarantee that the inmates' stories were better. No, I wouldn't be stopping the husks from getting to him.

Dar was on the interstate, sticking to what should have been the fastest route to South Dakota. Her route relied on maps; maps that were drawn up before the world went to shit and undead monsters clogged the streets. Most people would have done the same, which meant more abandoned cars, more blocked routes and a hell of a lot more husks. Local roads would add mileage, but I'd make up for lost time by avoiding all the other issues.

Having spent so long thinking I knew how this was going to end, I suddenly found myself uncomfortable with extending my time a little further. I wanted to go back to Brookview Cemetery, go back to Lisa and Kara. My phone was silent. I guess I had my answer.

"What's your deal, huh?" Frank asked.

I didn't want to answer or maybe it was that I didn't really know how. What the hell kind of question was that anyway? Who the fuck knew what their deal was?

"Were you a therapist on the outside or something?" I responded. I stared at the mattress hung above my own. The springs were tinged with rust or missing – just waiting to fall apart. Everything in here was the same. Even the people.

"Jeez, Lucas," Frank groaned. "You're just a fucking barrel of laughs. A master of dinner table conversation."

"Fuck you." I kicked the mattress above me with as much force as I could muster.

"Hey, man," Frank groaned. "I didn't mean to say anything about your family. My bad."

"Yeah. Whatever, don't stress it." I looked at the picture hanging on the wall. Lisa and Kara looked happy. I struggled to remember what that felt like.

"Still didn't need to put a foot in my ass," Frank continued. "I was just making small talk. That's what people do in here, you know? They talk all kinds of bullshit about what they'll do when they get out."

"When I get out?" I repeated.

"That is kind of the point," Frank said. "To get out. You need to have a plan, something to look forward to so you can muscle through the shit and survive."

"Gotcha." I didn't want to have this conversation. I didn't have a plan. My family was gone. What plan could I possibly make if they weren't part of it?

"So, like I said, what's your deal?" Frank leaned over the edge of his bunk and craned his head to see what I was doing. The motion caused a fart to escape. "What are you going to do when you get out?"

I stared at the wall, trying to ignore the stench. "When I get out? I'm going to see my family."

"Was that so hard?" Frank asked. "You gotta keep that image in your head, stay focused on seeing them again."

"Yeah, I guess you're right." Frank didn't know that Lisa and Kara were gone. He knew I was in here for trying to kill someone, but I never shared why. Kara and Lisa were dead and the thought of joining them was the only thing that was keeping me going.

-60-

Gray and orange. Everything was gray and orange. I spent years drowning in these colors, wanting nothing more than to never see them again, and now they appeared to be swallowing the world.

Cities burned in the distance as I traveled along abandoned stretches of highway. The gray skeletal remains of buildings scraped against black skies, ash and flame spilling from their shattered windows. The fires spread, illuminating the horrific scenes unfolding in the streets. Husks crawled from the buildings, writhing in the streets like desiccated maggots. Their grayed, weathered skin offered no contrast to the horrors that engulfed us. I couldn't tell if it was the heat, if some primal part of their brains still sensed the danger of fire, or if there was a meal nearby and it was simply the need to eat that called out to them.

I climbed back into the stupid-looking Hummer and got back on the road. There was no reason to waste time watching civilization's corpse burn.

This was Hell. For the first time since my release from prison, I found myself grateful that Kara and Lisa had been spared this nightmare. They were gone, but they would never have to know what a husk was or feel its yellowed, cracked teeth tear into their flesh. They had been spared. I was not so lucky. No matter. I knew where to find them when the time came.

For now, I had to find Danni and Jared. I didn't know if Jared had been bit back in the bunker or just hurt – either way he and Danni didn't have long. Time was short for everyone. The world had died and was slowly rotting. We were rotting. Only the dead would be spared from this fate.

Gray and orange. It seemed that I would never escape a world painted in these colors. Everything was gray and orange. As soon as I found Dar, I'd go about changing that, even if it was just a little, just a few feet of red concrete.

The End

CHECK OUT OTHER GREAT ZOMBIE NOVELS

Z BURBIA
by **Jake Bible**

Whispering Pines is a classic, quiet, private American subdivision on the edge of Asheville, NC, set in the pristine Blue Ridge Mountains. Which is good since the zombie apocalypse has come to Western North Carolina and really put suburban living to the test!

Surrounded by a sea of the undead, the residents of Whispering Pines have adapted their bucolic life of block parties to scavenging parties, common area groundskeeping to immediate area warfare, neighborhood beautification to neighborhood fortification.

But, even in the best of times, suburban living has its ups and downs what with nosy neighbors, a strict Home Owners' Association, and a property management company that believes the words "strict interpretation" are holy words when applied to the HOA covenants. Now with the zombie apocalypse upon them even those innocuous, daily irritations quickly become dramatic struggles for personal identity, family security, and straight up survival.

ZOMBIE RULES
by **David Achord**

Zach Gunderson's life sucked and then the zombie apocalypse began.

Rick, an aging Vietnam veteran, alcoholic, and prepper, convinces Zach that the apocalypse is on the horizon. The two of them take refuge at a remote farm. As the zombie plague rages, they face a terrifying fight for survival.

They soon learn however that the walking dead are not the only monsters.

CHECK OUT OTHER GREAT ZOMBIE NOVELS

900 MILES
by S. Johnathan Davis

John is a killer, but that wasn't his day job before the Apocalypse.

In a harrowing 900 mile race against time to get to his wife just as the dead begin to rise, John, a business man trapped in New York, soon learns that the zombies are the least of his worries, as he sees first-hand the horror of what man is capable of with no rules, no consequences and death at every turn.

Teaming up with an ex-army pilot named Kyle, they escape New York only to stumble across a man who says that he has the key to a rumored underground stronghold called Avalon..... Will they find safety? Will they make it to Johns wife before it's too late?

Get ready to follow John and Kyle in this fast paced thriller that mixes zombie horror with gladiator style arena action!

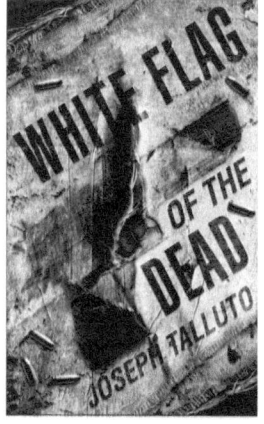

WHITE FLAG OF THE DEAD
by Joseph Talluto

Millions died when the Enillo Virus swept the earth. Millions more were lost when the victims of the plague refused to stay dead, instead rising to slaughter and feed on those left alive. For survivors like John Talon and his son Jake, they are faced with a choice: Do they submit to the dead, raising the white flag of surrender? Or do they find the will to fight, to try and hang on to the last shreds or humanity?

CHECK OUT OTHER GREAT ZOMBIE NOVELS

www.ingramcontent.com/pod-product-compliance
Lightning Source LLC
Chambersburg PA
CBHW051946170626
46808CB00007B/2503